"Without further delay, let me present our special guest, Mr. Justin Hayes, director of the new film *Denim Blues*," announced Mr. O'Brien, the principal of Maxwell High.

Mr. Hayes hadn't even set foot on the stage when the students went wild. They jumped to their feet, applauding and cheering. And to Chrissy's amazement, Caroline was just as excited as everyone else.

"It's really Justin Hayes!" Caroline said with enthusiasm. "Chrissy, you were right."

"Thank you, thank you very much," the director said quietly into the microphone at center stage. "I'm here to tell you about my latest project, *Denim Blues*. It's a young love-story that takes place here in beautiful San Francisco. We're working with an excellent script, and so far we've got a terrific cast, but we are still looking for two female co-stars. Now, I could just make some calls and sign up actresses who are already household names. But I'm not going to do that. I've decided that *Denim Blues* is the ideal vehicle to launch two unknowns. And that's why I'm here at your school. I'm looking for two special young women to co-star in *Denim Blues*."

"Me!" Chrissy shouted, jumping to her feet.

Other books in the **SUGAR & SPICE** series:

COMING SOON

Janet
Quin-Harkin's
Sugar & Spice

Make Me a Star

IVY BOOKS • NEW YORK

I'd like to thank
Susan Gorman
for all her help.

Ivy Books
Published by Ballantine Books
Copyright © 1988 by Butterfield Press, Inc. & Janet Quin-Harkin

Produced by Butterfield Press, Inc.
133 Fifth Avenue
New York, New York 10003

Library of Congress Catalog Card Number: 87-91004

ISBN 0-8041-0075-6

Manufactured in the United States of America

First Edition: February 1988

Make Me a Star

Chapter 1

"Cara! Wait up!" Chrissy Madden called down the hallway to her cousin. Her long blond hair streamed out behind her as she dodged the crowd of students in the corridor to reach Caroline.

"Calm down," Caroline said, shaking her head in amusement. "We're only going to a school assembly, not a Springsteen concert."

Chrissy could hardly contain her excitement. "From what I hear, this assembly will be just as good." She smiled mysteriously.

"What do you mean?" Caroline asked.

Chrissy pulled her cousin away from the crowd and into an empty doorway. "Well, Dolores Wright says that Justin Hayes was at her house for dinner last week and—"

1

"Wait a minute," Caroline interrupted. "You mean Justin Hayes, the movie director? What would he be doing having dinner at Dolores's house?"

"He went to college with Dolores's father," Chrissy whispered. "Anyway, he's making a movie right here in San Francisco starring Nick Matthews and Pete Becker. Dolores says he was asking her all kinds of questions about Maxwell High."

"So?"

Chrissy let out a long sigh of exasperation. "Don't you see, Cara? I bet he wants to use Maxwell as a location for the movie! Can you imagine—Nick Matthews and Pete Becker right here at Maxwell High?!"

"What about Nick Matthews and Pete Becker?"

Chrissy spun around to find her friend Tracy Wong standing behind her. "Hi, Tracy! I was just telling Cara that I've a hunch those two gorgeous actors are right here at Maxwell! I bet that's what the assembly is about." She grasped Tracy's arm with one hand and Caroline's arm with the other, and began pulling them down the hall toward the auditorium. "Come on! I want to get a good seat."

"Chrissy, don't you think your hunch is a little farfetched?" Caroline protested, pulling her arm away. "I wouldn't believe a word that Dolores Wright says."

In the middle of the hallway Chrissy stopped short and put her hands on her hips, nearly jabbing a passerby with her elbow. "Caroline

Kirby, don't be such a party pooper. I know Dolores tends to exaggerate, but even if it isn't true, just the thought of it helped me stay awake in every single class this morning."

With a grin, Tracy remarked, "Well, I'm glad of that, Chrissy, but somehow I think movie stars would be a little too busy to speak at a high school assembly." She turned to Caroline. "Did anyone mention this assembly at last week's student government meeting, Cara?"

"Not a word," Caroline replied. "Come on, you two, I want to stop at my locker on the way to the auditorium."

Reluctantly, Chrissy followed Caroline and Tracy down the hall and around the corner to Caroline's locker. She cringed as Caroline turned the combination on the lock. She knew her cousin would not be pleased when she opened the door.

"Chrissy, for goodness sake!" Caroline exclaimed, as a stack of miscellaneous school items tumbled from the locker. "You are such a slob. When I said you could put some of your stuff in my locker, I didn't mean for you to take it over."

"Sorry," Chrissy said, picking up a sweaty T-shirt and a pair of smelly socks.

"I'll bet the reason your mother wanted you to stay in San Francisco was so Danbury could have a chance to air out!" Tracy joked.

"Make that the whole state of Iowa," Caroline added in annoyance.

"I'm not that bad," Chrissy objected, trying to

stuff a sweat shirt onto the bottom shelf.

"Hey! What's this?" Tracy asked, picking up a magazine that had toppled out. She looked at the cover and sighed. "Pete Becker and Nick Matthews. Chrissy, you really are obsessed, aren't you? Where'd you get this?"

"At the library." Chrissy grinned. "You didn't think I ever went there, did you? You'd be amazed at what they have in the periodicals section." She took the magazine from Tracy and flipped through until she found the article about her latest heartthrob. "Listen to this, you two. 'Pete and Nick are now off to San Francisco to shoot their latest film, *Denim Blues*. Neither actor was at liberty to reveal the details of the plot, but we can tell you that with these two rising stars leading the cast, *Denim Blues* is sure to be a hit.'"

"That's enough about movie stars, Chrissy. You're driving me nuts," Caroline complained. She leaned over to rummage through all the junk in her locker. Finally, she pulled her math book out from under the mess. "You know, Chrissy, if you don't clean up this locker, you really will be seeing stars."

"Yeah, for all we know, Pete Becker and Nick Matthews could be trapped under your smelly old tennis shoes," Tracy said.

"Let me at them," Chrissy declared, making a mock dive toward the locker.

"Hopeless," Caroline said with a sigh. "Come on, we're going to be late for the assembly." With that, she swung the locker door shut, and the three girls merged with the crowd, making their way down the hall.

"I hope Justine or Maria saved us some seats. This place is packed," Caroline said, easing her way through the auditorium door.

"There's Justine," Tracy called, as she waved acknowledgment to the tall blonde across the room. She tucked her notebook under her arm and headed toward their friend.

"And it looks like she saved three places right down front," Chrissy added, bounding down the stairs two at a time. "Hey, Justine!" she said as she slid into the chair next to her friend. "Hi, Randy," she continued, greeting the boy sitting on Justine's other side. "What's up?"

"You'll never guess what," Justine began. "Randy swears he saw Justin Hayes walking backstage."

"Are you serious?" Tracy asked.

"It sure looked like him," Randy replied.

Chrissy grinned and turned to her cousin. "See, Cara? I was right! I bet Nick Matthews and Pete Becker are here, too."

"Honestly, Chrissy, what would they be doing here?" Caroline asked.

"Maybe they're scouting for new talent," Chrissy suggested, flipping her long blond hair and batting her twinkling blue eyes.

"Or maybe they got lost," Randy quipped as the lights dimmed and Mr. O'Brien, the principal of Maxwell High School, walked onstage.

"May I have your attention, please?" he called,

motioning with his hands for the crowd to be quiet. "We have some very special guests with us today, but before I bring them onstage, I want to remind you to be on your best behavior and show them the respect they deserve. I told them that the students at Maxwell were very nice, intelligent young men and women. Now don't let me down." He took a deep breath and glanced offstage. "So without further delay, let me present Mr. Justin Hayes, director of the new film *Denim Blues*."

Mr. Hayes hadn't even set foot on the stage when the students went wild. They jumped to their feet, applauding and cheering. And to Chrissy's amazement, Caroline was just as excited as everyone else.

"It's really Justin Hayes!" Caroline said with enthusiasm. "Chrissy, you were right."

"Thank you, thank you very much," the director said quietly into the microphone at center stage. "What a terrific reception. Thank you." He paused to allow the audience to calm down. "I'm here to tell you about my latest project, *Denim Blues*. It's a young-love story that takes place here in beautiful San Francisco. We're working with an excellent script, and so far we've got a terrific cast, but we are still looking for two female co-stars. Now, I could just make some calls and sign up actresses who are already household names. But I'm not going to do that." Mr. Hayes paused again and gazed out across the audience. "I've decided that *Denim Blues* is the ideal vehicle to launch two unknowns. And that's why I'm here at your school. I'm looking for two special young women to co-star in *Denim Blues*."

"Me!" Chrissy shouted, jumping to her feet.

"Chrissy, sit down!" Caroline hissed as she tugged on her cousin's bright pink sweat shirt.

All the students burst out laughing and Chrissy quickly sat back in her chair, her face nearly as pink as her shirt.

"Could be, young lady," Justin called, pointing to Chrissy, "and maybe your friend, too."

Out of the corner of her eye, Chrissy could see Caroline's face light up at Mr. Hayes's words. *Cara's as starstruck as I am*, she thought. *She just doesn't like to show it as much as I do.*

"I'm looking for two very dynamite gals," Mr. Hayes continued. "And I hope they're sitting somewhere in this crowd right here in front of me." He gestured dramatically toward the audience, where the students sat speechless. The gold ring on his finger glistened beneath the stage lights as he ran a suntanned hand through his hair. "I'm going to give every girl an opportunity to be seen. But I'm looking for a particular type, so if you think you're creative, energetic, hardworking, and you think you've got what it takes to be a star, show up here on Saturday morning at ten o'clock. Then if you get through the first cut, you'll have an audition with one of our two co-stars. I'll introduce them now—you've probably heard of them, the stars of *Denim Blues*, Pete Becker and Nick Matthews."

Suddenly the auditorium erupted in another loud burst of applause and cheers. Chrissy stood up so she could have a better view of the two actors as they walked out onstage. When she caught sight of them, she stopped clapping and simply stared. They were really there, right in front of her—and even better-looking in person!

Nick Matthews led the way. He had an air of confidence about him as he walked briskly toward the microphone and scanned the auditorium. Chrissy caught a glimpse of Nick's chocolate-colored eyes and inhaled deeply. Casually, he unbuttoned his sport jacket to reveal a muscular torso beneath a black T-shirt. *He must be the most gorgeous guy in the whole world,* Chrissy thought, letting her breath out slowly. *And to think I'll have a chance to star in a movie with him!*

Behind Nick, Pete Becker was smiling broadly. His hazel eyes were open wide with genuine pleasure at the reaction of the crowd, and when he shook his head good-naturedly, his light brown hair danced around his face.

"So I guess you have heard of us," Pete said laughingly into the microphone. The audience let out another burst of cheers.

"It's really great to be here—" Nick added.

"Especially to be here at Maxwell High," Pete interrupted. "Like Justin says, we're filming *Denim Blues* in San Francisco, and hopefully two of you girls will be in it, too."

"And don't be shy," Nick advised. "If you want a

chance to be in the movie, show up here on Saturday. This may be your big break!"

This was more than Chrissy could handle. In her mind she was already signing autographs. "This is it," Chrissy whispered to her cousin. "We wanted to do something awesome in our senior year, and this is it."

"It's not as easy as it looks," Caroline murmured back.

"I don't care what it takes. Besides, I really am nuts about Nick Matthews and Pete Becker, so that won't be acting."

Chrissy gazed dreamily at the two actors as they waved to the cheering crowd and left the stage. The lights in the auditorium came up full, and Chrissy, Caroline, and the others could hardly contain themselves.

"I can't believe this is happening," Tracy said quietly, blinking in disbelief.

"Are those two guys gorgeous, or what!" Chrissy sighed.

"They're not bad," Caroline admitted.

The others laughed.

"Not bad!" Chrissy exclaimed. She hit her head with the palm of her hand. "Holy mazoley! Cara, are you sure we're cousins?"

Caroline shrugged. "They're okay."

"Does that mean you're not going to audition?" Justine asked as they sidestepped through the seats to the center aisle.

"Oh, yes, she is," Chrissy announced, tugging on Caroline's linen jacket.

"Even I'm tempted to put on a wig and audition just so I can be in the movie," Randy said with a grin.

Justine took Randy's hand. "I'll tell you what I'll do," she began. "If I get a part, I'll put in a good word for you with Mr. Hayes."

"Gee, thanks, Justine," Randy replied sarcastically.

"Well, wild horses can't keep me from showing up on Saturday," Tracy said.

"I'm just not sure I'd have the time to act in the movie even if I wanted to," Caroline declared. "Besides, when I get into more advanced classes at The Acting Studio, I'll be auditioning for movies and plays all the time."

Chrissy gave her cousin a peculiar look, then shrugged. "Well, I came to San Francisco to experience all kinds of new things. I think acting in a movie with Pete and Nick fits my plans to a T." She paused. Then a huge smile spread across her face. "Can you imagine what everyone in Danbury will say about me being a movie star?"

"They'll probably put up a statue of you in the middle of a cornfield," Justine remarked.

"I'm serious," Chrissy said. "I could invite my whole family and all my friends to Hollywood for the premiere. I wonder if Ben would go," she mused. "He'd probably be jealous of all my fans," she added, giggling.

The group reached the auditorium door and stepped into the hallway.

"I've got to go this way," Tracy said, pointing to the left.

"Us, too," Justine and Randy said. "See you, Cara. 'Bye, Chrissy."

"Don't you want to audition?" Chrissy asked her cousin quietly when they were alone.

"It's not such a big deal," Caroline said, keeping her eyes on the floor as the girls walked briskly toward the hall where Chrissy's locker was located.

Chrissy gave her cousin a skeptical look. "Oh, come on, Cara. I bet you're just as excited as I am. You just have a weird way of showing it."

A small grin crossed Caroline's serious face. "You're the one who has a weird way of showing it, Chrissy, not me. You're the one who jumped up in the middle of the assembly."

"So what?" Chrissy replied. "Listen, Justin said he's looking for a specific type, and I think we're it."

"Justin?" Caroline questioned, stopping short. "You're calling him *Justin* now?"

"All right, all right," Chrissy conceded, pulling her cousin along. "I think that we are the type Mr. Hayes is looking for. You know—real California girls."

"But you're not a real California girl, remember? You're a real Iowa girl," Caroline reminded her. "Besides, acting is more than just being the right type. True performers study for years to prepare themselves for this career."

"Then you'll be that much better than the rest

of us," Chrissy replied as she hopped lightly around Caroline. "The class you've been taking at The Acting Studio puts you way ahead of the rest of us. Come on, you can't tell me you're not just a little bit intrigued."

"A little," Caroline confided as they reached Chrissy's locker.

"Which one do you like better—Nick Matthews or Pete Becker?" Chrissy asked as she twirled the combination. "I think Nick is incredibly gorgeous."

Caroline's grin grew wider. "Well, since you've obviously got your eye on Nick, I'll say Pete is cuter. They're both—" She paused, the grin vanishing from her face as she stared into Chrissy's locker. "Chrissy, how come there's hardly anything in your locker?" she asked sternly.

"Well . . . uh . . ." Chrissy hesitated, looking sheepish. Then her words tumbled out in a rush. "Most of my stuff is in your locker, Cara. It's so much closer to my classes—all except math, really—that it's much easier to keep my books and other junk in your locker. I'm sorry, Cara. You know you can put your stuff in my locker any time you want."

"Thanks, but, no, thanks," Caroline replied.

Chrissy pulled out her math book and slammed her locker shut. "Well, the offer's open," she said. "So, Cara, are you going to come on Saturday and see if you're the right type?"

"Maybe," Caroline answered. "But I would have to prepare myself properly."

"Does that mean you'll go on Saturday?" Chrissy asked hopefully.

Caroline was quiet for a moment. Then she said, "I'll make you a deal, okay?" Her face was stern, and Chrissy knew she meant business. "I'll show up Saturday."

"Great!" Chrissy started to interrupt.

"If," Caroline snapped, "you promise me something."

"Name it," Chrissy vowed.

"Promise me you'll clean your mess out of my locker."

"I promise, I promise," Chrissy agreed, twirling Caroline around. "We're going to be in the movie. I can just feel it."

"Don't get your hopes up too high," Caroline said as they headed toward the math department. "Like I said, it takes a lot of study and work to be an actress."

"I know, I know. That's why I'm going to need your help," she insisted. "You've been taking acting classes for a little while now. Could you give me a crash course before Saturday?"

"Chrissy." Caroline sighed, tossing her arms up in the air. "I wouldn't know where to begin. Acting isn't something you can learn overnight. And remember those "sophistication lessons" I gave you when you went out with Hunter? And the ballet lessons, total disaster!"

"I know, but this will be different. If you could give me a few pointers, then maybe I wouldn't make a fool of myself."

"All right, but you'll have to pay close attention. Trust me and do exactly what I tell you," Caroline instructed.

"You got it," Chrissy agreed as they sauntered into their math class. "We can start today after school," she added, sliding into the desk chair beside Caroline.

"We can start after you clean my locker," Caroline replied.

"You know, Cara," Chrissy hissed back, avoiding Mr. Turner's glare from the front of the room, "sometimes you're worse than my mother."

Throughout the hour Chrissy could hardly concentrate. She'd tucked the copy of *Teen Star* inside her trigonometry book and was staring into Nick Matthews's brown eyes. She memorized all his interests: surfing; old movies, especially James Dean movies; downhill skiing; skateboarding; and girls—not necessarily in that order. His favorite food: pepperoni pizza. Biggest turn-on: sunny days. Biggest turn-off: pollution. His ideal date would be a day at the beach, surfing in the ocean, and skateboarding on the boardwalk. It would end with a sunset over the waves and, of course, a good-night kiss . . . or two.

Or six or seven, Chrissy mused. She stared at the cover of her math book. On the cover someone had drawn a picture of a flower, which caught Chrissy's attention.

He loves me, he loves me not . . . she began as she made her way around the petals of the flower. *He loves me, he loves me not, he loves me!*

She reached the last petal and smiled to herself.

Perfect! Chrissy sighed contentedly.

Blue Denim would be a huge success, and she and Nick would be slated to do several more films together, all in exotic places like Tahiti, Paris, and Rome. But it would be the night of the Oscars in Los Angeles that he would pop the question. After they won the Academy Awards for best actress and actor, they would go to the fancy parties and be honored by their fans and peers. When all the publicity pictures and interviews were over, they would drive to the top of the Hollywood hills to watch the sun rise. As the last star disappeared from the horizon and the sky turned a bright shade of pink, he would kiss her tenderly and ask her to be his wife.

It would be the wedding of the century—even better than Princess Di's. Chrissy flipped open her notebook and began sketching her wedding gown. She'd want a lacy bodice with a long satiny skirt, and of course a train billowing out behind her as she walked down the aisle. . . .

"Miss Madden, that certainly is an interesting configuration, but all I asked for was a simple parallelogram."

Slowly, Chrissy laid her pencil on her desk and looked up. "Uh . . . Mr. Turner . . ." she stammered.

"Yes, that's me. I'm glad to see you've learned something in this class." Mr. Turner leaned closer to get a better look at Chrissy's sketch. "Hmm, are you practicing for a career in fashion design?"

Chrissy felt the hot blush envelop her face. She stared down at the tiled floor and didn't say anything.

"Well, Chrissy, I know you find trig boring," Mr. Turner continued, "but, believe me, it would be to your benefit to pay attention. It's amazing how fascinating triangles can be if you give them a chance." He looked around the room at the other students. "Right, class?" he said, nodding in answer to his own question.

Chrissy breathed a sigh of relief as Mr. Turner returned to the front of the room to continue the lesson. She could still hear the snickering of her classmates, but as she glanced across at her cousin, she was gratified to see Caroline's reassuring smile. Caroline gestured toward the blackboard, where Mr. Turner was drawing a series of figures. Although Chrissy tried to concentrate, all she could see was a vision of Nick Matthews floating before her.

I bet movie stars don't have to worry about stupid trigonometry, she thought.

Chapter 2

"My locker looks great," Caroline congratulated Chrissy later that afternoon.

"I decided to wait for you so we could walk home together, and I needed something to do while you were in student government," Chrissy replied. "Anything interesting going on? The meeting lasted longer than usual."

Caroline's heels clicked and Chrissy's rubber soles squeaked as they walked through the empty hallways.

"It's all talk about the movie." Caroline sighed.

"Really? What'd they say?" Chrissy asked, immediately perking up.

"Well, it's not going to be as easy as Mr. Hayes made it sound."

Chrissy's face immediately turned serious and

a boulder-sized lump lodged in her throat. "How do you mean?"

"The school board is insisting on some guidelines," Caroline said.

From the hesitation in her cousin's answer, Chrissy knew that the situation was bad. She stopped and took hold of Caroline's forearm. "What kind of guidelines?"

"Did you remember your trig notebook, Chrissy? I can't believe Mr. Turner gave us so much homework," Caroline said, pushing open the main door and walking out to the sidewalk.

"Quit trying to change the subject and tell me what happened at that meeting," Chrissy prodded as she quickened her step to catch up with her cousin. "I'm going to hear about it anyway, so I'd rather hear about it from you."

Again Caroline hesitated.

"Come on, Cara, tell me," Chrissy urged.

"Let's go up to the park and I'll explain it," Caroline suggested, turning to head up the hill toward the square where the girls and their friends ate lunch on sunny days.

"They're not going to let me audition because I'm from Iowa, is that it?" Chrissy asked, following on Caroline's heels.

"Don't be ridiculous."

"Only kids who have gone to Maxwell all four years will be looked at."

"Chrissy." Caroline sighed in exasperation.

"Is it because I'm too fat?"

"You're not too fat," Caroline said, sitting beneath bright pink rhododendron blossoms.

"Then what is it?" Chrissy demanded as she set her books on the ground and plopped down next to her cousin.

"All right, I'll tell you. It's nothing definite, so I really shouldn't be saying anything."

"Cara!" Chrissy shouted. "For Pete's sake, what is it?"

Caroline absentmindedly fixed the ribbon at the end of her long blond braid so that the bow was perfectly symmetrical. "Because of the three-month filming schedule, the school board is concerned about a student's scholastic development," she said.

"Huh?" Chrissy asked, scrunching her face in confusion. "What does that mean in English?"

"You can't just stop going to school for three months."

"I wouldn't," Chrissy answered, astonished. "But what's that got to do with being a movie star?"

"They want to make sure that whoever is picked will be able to keep up their grades, so they've decided that any student not maintaining an acceptable ranking in all of her classes can be eliminated by her teacher before Saturday's cuts." Caroline stared at Chrissy, who was staring back.

"What does this have to do with me?" Chrissy asked, thinking out loud. "I'd study twenty hours a day if I could spend the extra four hours filming the movie. Anyway, I should have an acceptable ranking. I'm getting A's and B's in all my courses except math, and Mr. Turner wouldn't . . ." Chrissy's brain stopped like a race car at a red light. She looked at Caroline, but her cousin averted her eyes.

"It's Mr. Turner, isn't it?" Chrissy's voice was barely audible.

Caroline nodded. "All the teachers turned in names of people who they think should be eliminated before Saturday, and your name was on Mr. Turner's list."

"That figures," Chrissy said, pulling a blossom off the rhododendron tree.

"I think your name was added to the list at the last minute," Caroline explained. "All the other kids' names were typed, but yours was written in pen."

"Did he have a reason?" Chrissy asked. She gazed down at the flower in her hand. It reminded her of the flower on the cover of her math book.

"He said you were tottering on a C in class now, and he thinks that if you get a part in the movie, you'll pay even less attention to math."

"All because of that stupid incident in class today." Chrissy dropped her flower and hugged her knees to her chest. In a way, she could see Mr. Turner's point, but it was her life, and if she considered the movie more important than trig, then that was her own business, wasn't it?

"Those lists are only preliminary, though, Chrissy," Caroline continued. "The teachers can change them any time until Friday morning."

"Do you think Mr. Turner might take my name off?" Chrissy asked, looking up hopefully.

"I sure do," Caroline replied, "but you've really got to prove to him that you're willing to put some effort into the class. I suggest you spend the next few days boning up on trig terms and raising your hand a lot in class discussion."

"You're right," Chrissy agreed. She stood up and squinted into the late-afternoon sun, then suddenly twirled around in a full circle with her arms stretched out at her sides. "Cara, you're absolutely right! By the end of the week I'm going to be a whiz at trig. Mr. Turner will have to take my name off the hit list. And then"—she paused to take a deep breath—"I just have to get past the first cuts on Saturday, audition with gorgeous Nick Matthews, then *shazam!* I'm a movie star!" She twirled around again, but this time she was off balance and landed in a heap in front of Caroline.

Caroline laughed and put her hand out to help up her cousin. "One thing I like about you, Chrissy, is your optimistic attitude."

"Thanks, Cara. You know what?" she asked, brushing the dirt off her jeans. "You are my very favorite cousin in the whole wide world."

Caroline put her hands on her hips and cocked her head. "All right, Chrissy Madden, what have you got up your sleeve?"

"Nothing," Chrissy protested. "Honest, Cara, I don't know why you think I'm always planning some harebrained scheme."

"Because you usually are," Caroline replied.

"I am not," Chrissy said, giving her cousin a mischievous grin. Then with one quick movement, she whipped the ribbon out of Caroline's hair and darted past her out of the park.

"Chrissy!" Caroline called out threateningly as she scooped up the books that Chrissy had left under the rhododendron tree. "You'd better get back here if you want your trig notebook. Mr. Turner won't be very happy if you lose it. Then your whole plan will go right down the drain!"

Out on the sidewalk, Chrissy did an about-face. *As usual, Cara's got a point there,* she thought, walking sheepishly back into the park. *Why does she always have to be so darned sensible?*

"Thanks," she said, taking her books from Caroline's outstretched hands.

"That's all right," Caroline replied as the girls headed out of the park together. "Do you want me to help you impress Mr. Turner? Believe it or not, I think I understand most of the stuff we've been learning in trig."

Chrissy's face lit up. "Would you, Cara? That'd be great."

"What are cousins for?" Caroline asked, then proceeded to explain the basics of trigonometry to Chrissy as they walked home.

"Hi, girls," Edith Kirby called, as Caroline opened the door to the Kirbys' third-floor apartment ten minutes later.

"Hi, Mom. You're home early," Caroline replied.

Her mother nodded. "Only because I said I'd put in some extra hours at the gallery on Saturday to set up a new exhibit."

"Oh, Aunt Edith, wait till you hear who was at school today," Chrissy burst out. "You'll never believe it!" She led the way into the kitchen and placed her books on the table with a thud.

Aunt Edith folded her arms across her chest and leaned against the counter. "Hmm, let's see . . . was it Mayor Feinstein?"

"Nope," Chrissy said, shaking her head. "I'll give you a hint. They are three very famous people from Hollywood."

"Don't tell me—The Three Stooges," Aunt Edith guessed.

"No, no, no," Chrissy said. She paused dramatically. "Justin Hayes, Pete Becker, and Nick Matthews!"

Aunt Edith smiled, obviously humoring her niece. "Holy mazoley! No kidding?" she said, imitating Chrissy. "Were they putting on a concert or something?"

"Mom, Justin Hayes is a movie director, and Pete and Nick are actors," Caroline said, patting her mother's shoulder. "Nice try, though."

"Cara and I are going to be in a film with them right here in San Francisco," Chrissy declared.

"Is that so?" Aunt Edith said, turning to give her daughter a questioning look.

"Well, it's a little more complicated than that," Caroline said, taking a seat at the table. "First we have to be the right types and audition and pass math." She emphasized the word *math* and glared in Chrissy's direction.

"Caroline promised to help me with my math homework," Chrissy added nervously, "and give me some acting lessons."

"They'll be sending special release forms to the parents if we pass the first step," Caroline reassured her mother. "So, you don't have to worry about anything until then."

"I'm not worried," Mrs. Kirby said. "I trust your good judgment. After all, you girls are seniors now—almost adults. Just remember to mention me in your acceptance speeches when you both win Academy Awards," she added as she left the room.

"Okay, where do we start?" Chrissy asked, opening the refrigerator and taking out two apples. She tossed one to Caroline and took a bite from the other. "Do you have a practice scene we could try? Some Shakespeare, maybe? 'Oh, Romeo, Romeo, wherefore art thou, Romeo?'" she cried, throwing her arms out in a dramatic gesture.

"Get your math book," Caroline said, taking a crunchy bite of her apple. "You need to bone up some more for class tomorrow."

"Couldn't I just practice balancing it on my head?" She picked up the book and balanced it carefully on top of her golden tresses. "Hey! Maybe I can learn this stuff by osmosis."

"Fat chance." Caroline smirked, stretching a hand out to tickle her cousin.

Chrissy yelped in surprise and wriggled away from Caroline's reach, causing the book to slip off her head.

"Time to get serious and see if you remember anything I taught you on the way home," Caroline said.

"Yes, ma'am," Chrissy said, giving her cousin a military-style salute. "The longest side of a right triangle is called a hypo-noose," she began.

"Hypotenuse," Caroline corrected.

Chrissy munched on her apple. "That's what I said. Anyhow, an acute angle is less than ninety degrees, right?" Caroline nodded. "And an obtuse angle is greater than ninety degrees," Chrissy added, taking a last bite of her apple, then throwing it into the garbage can as if tossing a basketball. "Two points!" she said.

Caroline applauded. "Very good! I'm impressed."

"With what—my amazing athletic ability or my terrific intelligence?" Chrissy asked with a grin.

"Both. But at the moment I'm more interested in your intelligence. I think Mr. Turner will be impressed."

Suddenly serious, Chrissy flopped down in the chair across from Caroline. "I sure hope so," she said with a sigh.

Chapter 3

"C squared equals A squared plus B squared,"
Chrissy mumbled to herself early the next morning as she pulled on her red corduroy skirt. "The
hypotenuse squared equals the square of one
side plus the square of the other side."

That's not so hard, she thought. *I don't know
why I didn't understand it before.*

She slipped her gold cardigan sweater on top of
a matching plaid blouse with a ruffled collar, then
pulled her hair back into a ponytail with a ribbon
from Caroline's dresser.

Not bad, she decided, analyzing her image in
the mirror. *I look as brainy as I feel. Maybe this
outfit will make people take me more seriously. It
had better have that effect on Mr. Turner!* she
thought. Who'd have thought a dumb math

teacher could stand in the way of her career as a famous movie star?

With a deep sigh, Chrissy sat at her desk and opened her math book. Although it was only six o'clock, and no one else would be up for at least another hour, Chrissy had risen early for some last-minute studying. The night before, Caroline had explained equations and formulas until she was blue in the face, and the girls had stayed up an extra three hours preparing Chrissy for her battle with Mr. Turner.

Now as she reviewed Caroline's lessons, she was truly amazed at how simple trig could be once she put her mind to it. *Common sense, that's all it is,* she told herself. *No wonder Caroline is so good at trig. And thanks to her patient tutoring, I'm going to knock the socks off Mr. Turner! Then I'm going to star in* Denim Blues *with Pete Becker and . . .* Chrissy felt a thrill at the mere mention of his name. "Nick Matthews," she whispered, closing her eyes dreamily.

From across the room, she heard a rustling sound, and she opened her eyes to see Caroline turning over in her bed.

Cara's been really great to help me so much, Chrissy thought. *I know! Why don't I surprise her with breakfast in bed?*

She shut her book quietly, then tiptoed down the hallway to the kitchen. "I'll start with fresh-squeezed orange juice and coffee," she said, scurrying around the kitchen preparing Caroline's breakfast. It wasn't Chrissy's idea of a

hearty meal, but she was sure her cousin would
love it. Caroline and her parents ate a whole
different way than her own family. A good breakfast back home wouldn't be complete without at
least half a dozen flapjacks, eggs, and bacon or
sausages. And her mother's blueberry muffins
and homemade preserves—*mmm!*

For a moment Chrissy felt homesick. She wondered how her brothers were faring at Uncle
Ned's. And how were the repairs coming along
on the farm? *That tornado really must have been
something to cause so much damage,* she
thought. *At least no one was hurt, but I guess
everything will be different when I get home,
what with rebuilding the house and all.*

"Home." She sighed. "Funny how this apartment feels so much like home these days. I guess
I'll really have to get used to city living if I'm
going to be a movie star," she said aloud to
herself. "I suppose not too many film stars live on
farms in Iowa."

Chrissy turned on the coffee maker, then
squeezed some oranges into a pitcher. She
grabbed some fresh fruit out of the lower bin of
the refrigerator and began slicing the bananas,
apples, and strawberries into a dish, preparing
enough for Uncle Richard and Aunt Edith, too.

With each task, she reviewed all she'd learned
about trigonometry. She almost wished she could
run over to Mr. Turner's house and prove to him
right then how much she knew, so she could get
it over with and calm her nerves. Instead, she

took a large container of plain yogurt and folded the sliced fruit into the creamy mixture. Then she got down a bright blue breakfast tray from the top shelf of a nearby cabinet. On it she arranged the coffee, juice, and fruit-and-yogurt mixture, along with a neatly folded napkin and a spoon. Carefully, she balanced the tray on her arms and walked back down the hall to her and Cara's room. She could hear Uncle Richard doing his morning exercises, with Aunt Edith pretending to act like his drill sergeant. The day was starting off wonderfully, Chrissy thought. She pushed open the bedroom door with her foot, spilling only the tiniest bit of orange juice. "Good morning, sleepy-head," she called cheerfully to the mound of covers that was her cousin.

"What time is it?" Caroline grumbled, rolling over and reaching for her alarm clock.

"Time to rise and shine," Chrissy answered, "to another beautiful day in California."

"Ugh! I can't handle this much happiness in the morning. Call me when you're finished in the shower."

"I've been finished in the shower for over an hour," Chrissy practically sang as she placed the tray on Caroline's night table. "Come on, sit up. I have a surprise." She tossed her pillow in the air and fluffed it before placing it behind Caroline's head.

"My eyes aren't functioning correctly yet," Caroline groaned, easing herself into a sitting position, "but my nose definitely smells fresh coffee."

"Bingo!" Chrissy cheered, circling around the foot of the bed. "And yogurt with fruit and fresh-squeezed O.J."

"What's the occasion?" Caroline asked, rubbing her eyes. "I know it's not my birthday."

"It's just my way of saying thanks. You really went out of your way to help me last night, and since I doubt that there's any subject I could help you with, I figured breakfast in bed was the next-best thing." She lifted the tray and positioned it on Caroline's lap. "Ta-da!"

"This looks wonderful, Chrissy!" Caroline exclaimed. "I'll tutor you any time you ask if it means I'll get this royal treatment."

"You know, I remember most of what you taught me, too," Chrissy said, sitting at the foot of Caroline's bed. "And look, what do you think of my outfit?" she asked, jumping up and taking a quick spin.

"Careful," Caroline said, reaching for her orange-juice glass. She motioned for Chrissy to spin around again and then took a sip of her juice. "Very conservative, Chrissy. You look like you're aiming for the Ivy League. Familiar-looking bow you have in your hair, by the way."

"I know, I should have asked first. Do you mind?"

"Not a bit," Caroline said, smiling. "Now, if you can sound as intelligent as you look, Mr. Turner will have to agree to your audition."

"I hope so," Chrissy answered, crossing her fingers. "I'm going to go have my breakfast and study some more. Let me know when you're ready to go. And thanks again for everything, Cara."

By eight-fifteen the girls were walking toward school and Chrissy's confidence had turned to apprehension. Normally when she was nervous, she babbled on nonstop, but today she was quiet.

The fall morning was crisp and the air fresh with the smell of the ocean. The curving hills bustled with the sounds of people on their way to work—cable cars clanged, horns tooted, and thousands of feet pounded the sidewalk. *Everyone looks so sure of where they're going*, Chrissy thought. *All hustle and bustle. Life on the farm is nothing like this.* She'd had a hard time trying to describe to her Iowa friends what it was like living in San Francisco. Places like Fisherman's Wharf, Chinatown, and the Golden Gate Bridge had to be experienced firsthand.

"Want me to quiz you for a while?" Caroline asked, breaking the silence.

"No, thanks, Cara. You've helped me more than enough. I'm going to review right before class and hope for the best."

Caroline stopped at the bottom of the hill and looked at her cousin with a new respect. "I'm really proud of you, Chrissy," she said. "And I've decided that if old man Turner won't let you try out for the movie, I'm not going to do it either. It just wouldn't be any fun without you."

Chrissy could feel a lump growing in her

throat. She was so lucky to have Caroline for a cousin. Caroline's faith and friendship meant more than any movie. "If I can't try out, you'll have to do the movie for both of us," she said firmly.

"Nope." Caroline shook her head. "Anyway, you're going to knock Mr. T's socks off today, so we won't worry about it," she declared, giving Chrissy a quick hug.

Once at school, Chrissy got caught up in the activities of the morning, but as math class loomed closer, her anxiety increased. Finally, she decided that for the sake of her sanity, she should put all thoughts of trigonometry to the back of her mind until she walked through the door of Mr. Turner's classroom; otherwise, she'd be in such a nervous state that she was sure to mess up.

"Hey, Chrissy!"

Startled, Chrissy turned around to see a small dark-haired girl running down the hall toward her.

"Hi, Maria," Chrissy greeted her friend. "Gee, it's too bad you missed the assembly yesterday. I guess you heard all about it."

"I didn't miss it," Maria said, smiling. "I got back from my dentist appointment just in time. Which reminds me!" she exclaimed. "Tracy told me about those magazines you had, and I went to the school library to take a look at those articles on Pete Becker and Nick Matthews, but the librarian said you had them all."

"Is that so?" Chrissy feigned surprise.

"Yeah. So how about spreading the wealth a bit?" Maria added, putting her hands on her hips.

"I'll make you a deal," Chrissy offered. "You can have the magazine of your choice for the weekend, if you'll let me borrow your red hightop sneakers for Saturday. They're just what I need to make Justin Hayes notice me."

Maria shrugged. "Sure, you can wear them. I can't imagine that they'd impress Mr. Hayes, but I'll bring them to school tomorrow."

"Great," Chrissy replied as the girls rounded the corner and entered their English class together. *Now let's just pray I have a reason to use them*, she thought.

Chrissy felt as if half the afternoon had passed before the bell finally rang, signaling the end of class. Now the time had come. The route to Mr. Turner's classroom was long and endless. With every step she took, the hallway seemed to stretch longer and longer. She felt as if she'd never get there on time, and then Mr. Turner would blackball her for sure. Her brain was like mush—she only hoped she could stay coherent for another hour. After a long, deep breath and a smile of encouragement from Caroline, who was waiting for her at the door, Chrissy entered the lion's den. She took her seat and looked straight ahead without speaking to anyone.

"Before we start work on the problems from Chapter Five, does anyone have any questions?"

Mr. Turner began, rolling a piece of chalk between his hands.

Chrissy sat taller in her chair and concentrated on his every word.

"All right, let's review, then. Who can tell me who is known as the father of geometry?" he asked.

Chrissy shot up her arm like a missile and hoped he would call on her.

"Chrissy," Mr. Turner called, somewhat surprised.

"René Descartes," Chrissy answered, quickly blurting out the name, as if afraid she might forget it.

"That's correct. Now, can anyone tell me the definition of an isosceles triangle?"

Once again, Chrissy raised her hand and answered the question correctly. For the next sixty minutes, Chrissy raised her hand to answer questions. She felt like a contestant on a game show, and with each correct answer her confidence grew. It was even kind of fun, she thought. To her pleasure, at the end of the hour, she had answered eight questions correctly.

For the rest of the week, Chrissy kept up her performance in math class, answering at least half a dozen questions every day, and paying close attention to everything Mr. Turner said. By Friday, she felt like an expert mathematician.

"Class dismissed," Mr. Turner announced at the end of Thursday's class. "Chrissy, may I speak with you for a moment, please?"

"Hang in there," Caroline whispered as she passed her cousin on her way out. "You were great. He's got to let you try out for the movie now."

Chrissy stood up slowly and noticed how stiff she felt. She hadn't shifted positions once during the hour and her tension grew as she approached Mr. Turner's desk.

"First, I would like to apologize to you about Monday's incident," Mr. Turner said softly. Chrissy's eyes widened and she held her breath. "I was a little hard on you, but I get very frustrated when I feel a bright student isn't taking advantage of her opportunities and potential. I must say that for the past few days, however, you've been proving that I was wrong about you."

Chrissy felt herself relax.

"I'm enormously pleased by your improvement, but I get the feeling that the only reason you've turned over a new leaf is so you can have a crack at being in that movie," Mr. Turner added, looking directly at Chrissy and making her feel uncomfortable. "Am I right?"

Hesitating, Chrissy averted her eyes and cleared her throat. "That's partly true," she admitted. "I do want to be in the movie, and that's what gave me the original motivation to work harder at trig. But once Cara helped me learn the basics, I found that trig wasn't so hard after all."

Mr. Turner smiled, and, to Chrissy's surprise, he actually looked like an ordinary person, instead of a mean old teacher. "I'm glad we've had this talk, Chrissy," he said. "If you promise me you'll continue to spend your time in this class working on math, I think I can feel good enough to take your name off the list."

"Really?" Chrissy cried, trying to stand on her wobbly legs. "I won't let you down, I promise." She gathered up her books and headed for the exit. "Thank you, thank you very much," she added, grinning from ear to ear. She pushed open the door and burst into the hallway to find Caroline waiting for her.

Before her cousin could say a word, Chrissy spun her around and cheered. "I've done it!" she cried. "Tomorrow, Cara, you and I are going to show Mr. Hayes exactly what types he's looking for to star in the movie. I wonder if Nick Matthews will be there. . . ." she added, her blue eyes opening wide in anticipation. "Hollywood, here we come!"

Chapter 4

"Chrissy, hurry up, we're going to be late," Caroline called from the bathroom the next morning.

"I know, I know," Chrissy answered, throwing another blouse on her bed. "I can't decide what to wear."

"But you've been trying on different outfits all week." Caroline poked her head into the room and gasped. "This place is a disaster area."

"It's just that I'm having a little difficulty making up my mind." Chrissy groaned as she tried to snap on a pair of tight pants. "I can't believe these don't fit. I'm going to be too fat to be chosen as the right type." Chrissy peeled off the pants and threw them on the pile.

"Hey! This is mine!" Caroline exclaimed, rescuing a blue tweed blazer from the mound.

Suddenly Chrissy's eyes lit up. "I've got it!" she exclaimed, snatching the coat from Caroline's hands and tucking it under her arm. She scavenged through the pile on the bed and pulled out a denim miniskirt. Sliding it over her blue-gray tights, she hopped to the closet and plucked out a blue oxford blouse she'd borrowed from Justine. "You don't think Uncle Richard will mind if I borrow his skinny black tie, do you?" she asked Caroline, rushing past her and into her aunt's and uncle's room.

"Does it really matter what I say?" Caroline muttered just loud enough for Chrissy to hear.

But Chrissy was too excited to pay any attention. "Ta-da!" Chrissy said, posing in their doorway, waiting for approval. "What do you think? Am I a hip teen-ager of the eighties, or what!"

"I vote for the 'or what,'" Caroline replied, as she flopped on her bed. "Actually, it's not half bad, except you're not wearing one article of clothing that belongs to you."

"Sure I am," Chrissy said, inspecting her ensem-ble.

"The hightop sneakers are Maria's; the red socks are Randy's; the tights and jean skirt are mine; the blouse is Justine's; the red belt is Mom's; and the tie is Dad's. If you're chosen the right type, you're going to have to share your part with a lot of other people."

"Very funny." Chrissy sighed. "Maybe I should change into something else."

"No, no way," Caroline said, lying back on her

pillow. "The audition is at ten o'clock, and it's nine-thirty already. We'd better leave now. I'm sure every girl from Maxwell will be there."

"Well, you'd better hurry, then, and get ready yourself," Chrissy said.

"I *am* ready." Caroline jumped up and confronted her cousin. "What's wrong with the way I look?"

"It's a little conservative, don't you think?" Chrissy replied, circling Caroline.

"You're the one who is wearing the coat and tie. I'm at least wearing a dress."

"Yeah, but it's drab green."

"Khaki color is in style, Chrissy. And besides, I think using the print scarf as a belt is very vogue."

Chrissy shrugged. "Suit yourself. It's just that Mr. Hayes is probably looking for someone who really stands out from the crowd."

"Like you, I suppose?" Caroline asked with a note of sarcasm.

"I wasn't going to say anything, but now that you mention it," Chrissy replied, straightening her tie, "yes."

"At least I look like me, because I'm wearing my own clothes," Caroline countered. "Discussion over. We have to leave now if we're going to get there before tomorrow."

After a last touchup in front of the mirror, the girls rushed downstairs.

"Let's take a cab," Chrissy suggested, "and act like real movie stars."

"Chrissy, the school is only a few blocks away," Caroline objected, already walking down the hill. "And besides, neither of us can afford it."

Chrissy hurried to catch up with her cousin. "But just think, Cara, pretty soon we'll be starring in a smash movie. Then we'll be making tons of money."

"Don't jump the gun," Caroline warned. "Let's see if we pass this first step."

The girls continued walking briskly along, each lost in her own thoughts.

"How can you always be so confident?" Caroline asked suddenly.

Looking at her cousin's intent expression, Chrissy had to smile. "I'm not so confident—I just act like I am," she said. "If I act confident on the outside, it makes me feel better on the inside. I'll let you in on a secret, though; I don't feel so confident now, and I want to be in this movie so badly!"

As Chrissy finished speaking, she spotted a long line of girls standing outside the school. "Holy cow!" She gasped.

There had to be at least two hundred girls in the line that wound past the main entrance and around to the gym.

"Where did all these girls come from?" Chrissy wondered aloud.

"They all have the same idea as we do. We might as well get in line with the rest of the cattle," Caroline said.

"Maybe we can find Justine and Maria."

Chrissy and Caroline wove their way through the crowd. About halfway through the pack, Justine and Maria were standing, waiting their turn.

"Can you believe this?" Justine asked, motioning at the crowd.

"We must be crazy to want to do this," Maria grumbled. "Maybe Tracy had the right idea when she said it would be useless."

Caroline shrugged. "It's worth a try. Come on, Chrissy," she said, pulling the sleeve of Chrissy's jacket. "We'd better go to the back before this mob gets any bigger."

Reluctantly, Chrissy agreed, and she followed Caroline to the end of the line. They had been waiting only a short time, when two young men wearing official-looking badges stepped on a platform outside the gym doors.

"Good morning, girls," the one with the reddish hair announced through a bullhorn. "We'll be starting in about five minutes, so be patient." He grinned, revealing a wide, friendly smile. "Whoever gets chosen will have to get used to waiting. When you make a film, waiting around on the set takes up about seventy-five percent of your time."

As they waited the extra five minutes, Chrissy took note of the other guy on the platform. With his blue eyes, sun-streaked hair, moustache, and his tall, muscular physique, Chrissy thought he looked like a Greek god.

"We're going to start now," the redhead said

into the horn, to the applause and cheers of all the girls. "Please walk into the gym ten at a time and stand on the center line. No talking and no changing positions. Each girl will have an equal opportunity. If Mr. Hayes chooses you to read from the script, you will be given a green card to fill out and return to Josh. He's the big guy here."

The girls all giggled and the Greek god flexed his muscles. "One last thing," the redhead continued. "Remember we're looking for a specific type. If you're not chosen, don't be upset. It doesn't mean we don't like you. It simply means you're not what we want for this particular film. Okay, let's get started with the first ten gals."

Chrissy and Caroline looked at each other in anxious anticipation and Chrissy gave her cousin's hand a quick squeeze. She could tell that Caroline was tense by the strained expression on her face. Her own stomach was doing flip-flops and her skin felt too tight for her body. Chrissy scanned the crowd and tried to figure out who and what they might be looking for.

"That didn't take long," Caroline said quietly as the first group of ten filed out of the gym.

"They don't look too happy," Chrissy commented. "There's only one girl holding a green card."

I just have to get a green card, she thought. *This is my chance to make it big. I know I could be a really great actress—everyone's always saying how dramatic I am. But what if Mr. Hayes isn't looking for a girl with long blond hair? Or blue eyes? Or big feet?* Chrissy knew she could go on forever, but if Mr. Hayes didn't want her the way she was, there wasn't much she could do about it.

She closed her eyes, took a deep breath, and prayed that Mr. Hayes was looking for a blonde with blue eyes and big feet.

"Excuse me. Are you all right?"

Chrissy heard the deep male voice, but she didn't think he could be talking to her—until she felt a light poke in the ribs. She opened her eyes to find Caroline giving her a look of exasperation, while Josh the Greek god was giving her a look of concern.

"Are you all right?" he asked again.

Chrissy couldn't help staring into Josh's clear blue eyes. "Y-yes, I'm f-fine," she stammered.

But Josh had already motioned to the redhead up on the platform. "Hey, Adam," he called, "can you get this girl a can of soda from the machine inside?"

A minute later, Adam rushed from the gym with a cool drink for Chrissy.

"Here you go," he said breathlessly, handing her the can.

"Thanks," she said, accepting it gratefully. "Thanks." Although she wasn't as ill as they seemed to think, Chrissy still appreciated the drink. It helped to calm her nerves, and now that she felt a bit better, she was enjoying the attention.

"Are you feeling okay now?" Josh asked. "I was

worried we had a casualty on our hands."

"There's no need to worry about Chrissy," Caroline muttered.

Ignoring her cousin, Chrissy put on her best smile. "Oh, yes, I'm fine now, thank you."

Josh breathed a sigh of relief. "Oh, good." Then he grinned at Adam. "I bet Justin would have loved the publicity, though."

"Yeah. I can just see the headline: 'Girl Faints at *Denim Blues* Casting Call—Director Hayes Hires Her . . .'"—Adam glanced at Caroline—"'. . . and Her Friend,'" he added quickly.

"Wouldn't that be great!" Chrissy sighed wistfully, noticing that even Caroline had smiled at that. "Are you guys both in the movie?" she asked.

"Not quite," Josh answered.

"I'm a film student at Berkeley," Adam put in, "and I'm doing an internship as Justin's personal assistant while he's filming in San Francisco."

"And I'm sort of a right-hand man for Pete and Nick," Josh began.

Chrissy's eyes opened wide in awe. "Really? So you know them personally?"

Josh laughed. "Yeah. I work as their bodyguard when they go out, fending off photographers and protecting them from overzealous fans." He gave Chrissy an amused glance, as if to say that he knew she was one of those overzealous fans. "I do errands and things, and right now," he added, "I'm teaching Nick to skateboard for some scenes in the movie."

"No kidding. Wow!" Chrissy remarked, even more impressed. "I've always wanted to learn how to skateboard, and to think you're coaching Nick Matthews!"

"I could coach you, too, if you want," Josh offered. "I don't have much time at the moment, though, but maybe when I have a little time off."

"That'd be great!" Chrissy enthused. Just then she noticed another group of ten girls leaving the gym, but she didn't see any of them carrying a green card. Suddenly she realized that striking up a friendship with Josh could have an extra advantage. Caroline was chatting away with Adam, it seemed she had the same thought in mind.

"How many girls do you think Mr. Hayes will choose?" Chrissy asked Josh, pretending to act casual, even though her insides had started churning again. "Do you know what type of girls he's looking for?"

"I don't really know about the type," Josh replied, "but I suspect Justin will have about twenty-five or fifty come back."

"Is that all?" Chrissy gasped.

"Now, don't get worried. You two should have a good chance. You should be in one of the next few groups, so just relax." Josh glanced at his watch. "Oops! We'd better get back inside."

Adam nodded. "Maybe we'll see you later," he added. The fellows walked toward the entrance, and Chrissy turned to Caroline.

"I think I'm more nervous now than ever," she

confessed. "From what Josh said, Mr. Hayes is only picking about fifteen percent of the girls here to audition. That's not much." Nervously, she paced along the sidewalk, biting her nails. "We've got to do something."

"Calm down," Caroline ordered, grabbing hold of Chrissy's arm. "Adam said everyone will have a chance, and besides, Josh wasn't even sure of the exact number."

"We've just *got* to be chosen," Chrissy said desperately.

"Look, there's Justine and Maria coming out now." Caroline waved to her friends, who ran over to join the cousins. "How did it go?" Caroline asked.

"They gave me a green card!" Justine shouted. "Next Saturday I'll get to do a scene with Pete or Nick."

"What about you, Maria?" Chrissy asked. "Did you get a green card, too?"

Maria shook her head, sighing dreamily. "Nope," she said, "but I don't care." She held her hand up in front of her dazed expression.

"What happened to you?" Caroline asked, snapping her fingers in front of Maria's eyes.

"You tell them, Justine, I'm still in shock," Maria whispered.

"Nick Matthews came up to her inside the gym and shook her hand," Justine told the girls.

"And he said I was the foxiest thing he'd seen all day," Maria added. "I'll never wash this hand again."

Justine grinned. "I thought she was going to faint."

"Is Pete Becker in there, too?" Caroline was obviously trying to sound nonchalant, but Chrissy detected a note of unexpected interest.

"Oh, yes," Justine replied. "He's standing to one side looking as handsome as ever. Oh, how I love those strong silent types."

Chrissy noticed a quick smile cross her cousin's face. Clearly, Caroline wasn't as cool and detached about these movie stars as she pretended.

"Keep the line moving, ladies," Adam interrupted, motioning for Caroline to move along. "You're in the next group."

Chrissy's heart started pounding harder and faster. Her time had nearly come! *I've just got to make a good impression,* she thought as she stared intently at the gym door. Adam came out of the gym and set his clipboard down on the step while he gave directions to one of the other girls. Curious, Chrissy sat quietly on the step to take a look. *It's a schedule for filming,* of course, Chrissy thought as she scanned the top page marked "Extras." Underneath it were times and locations of the next few days' shooting schedule. Her eyes caught the entry for the following afternoon:

Sunday 3:00 at the Japanese tea garden, Golden Gate Park.

"Let's go, Chrissy," Caroline said as Adam called

their group into the gymnasium. Chrissy darted
back to her place in line behind Caroline and
walked through the gym's expansive double
doors. Nervously, the girls marched down the
center line, as they had been instructed. On one
side of the bleachers, a long table and several
chairs had been set up. Immediately, Chrissy
recognized Justin Hayes sitting in the center,
flanked by Pete and Nick and four other people
whom Chrissy didn't know. She turned with the
other girls to face the panel, trying not to let her
knees shake.

The panel whispered among themselves for a
minute, and then Justin spoke.

"You, there, in the green dress. What's your
name?"

"Me?" Caroline gasped, taking a look around
her. "My name is Caroline. Caroline Kirby."

Chrissy was stunned. Caroline? Why would Mr.
Hayes choose Caroline and not her? She knew
she shouldn't be jealous, but she couldn't help it.
After all, she was the one who wanted to be in
the movie more than almost anything.

Suddenly she heard Mr. Hayes say, "And you,
next to Caroline, with the tie, take a green card,
too."

"Oh, thank you, Mr. Hayes!" Chrissy cried out
with glee.

Mr. Hayes's smile held a touch of impatience.
"So I want you both to come back two weeks
from today to audition with our two stars here,"

he said, nodding to Pete and Nick, on either side of him.

Chrissy looked at the two actors and breathed in deeply. *It's true! I've made it! Look out, Hollywood, Chrissy Madden is on her way!* she thought. As she gazed at Pete and Nick, Nick grinned and winked one velvety brown eye. Chrissy was sure it was meant just for her, and her heart flipped over.

"That will be all for now," Justin announced. The other girls in the group frowned in disappointment. "Thank you for taking the time to come to this call. We hope you'll all come to the movie when it's released. Caroline and the girl with the tie, we'll see you again soon. Adam Dawson will give you more information."

"We're in!" Chrissy exploded as she and Caroline exited the gym. Justine, Maria, and Randy were waiting outside for the news.

"I'm the only one who isn't auditioning," Maria said, laughing. "But don't worry, I'm not upset. I have a lifetime of daydreams resting on this hand. Besides, I honestly don't think I could go through another session like today's. I've had three anxiety attacks already." The gang all chuckled and congratulated one another on their success.

"I'm going to go over and find out what we need to do for the audition," Caroline said, noticing Adam sitting on the edge of the platform.

"What'd I tell ya!" he said to Caroline as she approached, with Chrissy right behind her. "You two girls passed with flying colors."

"But that's only the first step," Caroline reminded him. "What happens next?"

"It's really very simple," he explained. "You'll have a scene to look over, and you'll read it with one of the guys."

Chrissy nodded. That was pretty much what she'd expected. "Is there any way I can read with Nick?" she asked.

"Chrissy, don't you think that Mr. Hayes will want to decide that?" Caroline remarked.

"Maybe, but there's no harm in asking, is there?" she replied, turning to Adam.

"I'll see what I can do," he answered with an amused smile. "Here are your packets. Read them carefully. They have all the information you'll need to know. My phone number is on the top if you have any questions, and the address of the audition is listed on the bottom."

"Thanks a lot," Caroline said. "You've been a big help to both of us."

"Yeah, thanks," Chrissy added, "and tell Josh I'm ready for those skateboard lessons whenever he is." The girls watched Adam join the rest of the crew, then left the school with high hopes.

"Holy mazoley!" Chrissy said happily on the way home. "Who'd have thought a farmer's daughter from good old Danbury, Iowa, would become a movie star!"

Caroline laughed. "You're not a movie star yet, Chrissy. We've got to do this audition next week." She opened up the packet Adam had given her and took out the top sheet. "Chrissy, listen to this summary of the plot. It sounds really good!" She stopped on the sidewalk and began to read. " 'Eddie Davis'—that's Nick—'and Kevin Webster'—that's Pete—'have been best friends ever since they can remember. Trouble starts when Eddie becomes interested in Shannon, a girl who simply won't conform to please anyone—not even Eddie, but that's one of the reasons he likes her so much. His sister, Julie, is dead set against the relationship, so she and Kevin team up to bring Eddie back to his senses. But Julie and Kevin end up falling in love themselves, as they gradually come to understand the sense in Eddie's relationship with Shannon.' "

By the time Caroline had finished reading, Chrissy was fairly bursting with excitement. "Oh, Cara, what a terrific story! And the roles are perfect—you can be Julie, and I'm Shannon. It's as if the movie was written just for us. Now we absolutely have to get the parts!" she shouted, racing down the hill. With her arms open wide, she felt as if she were flying.

Chapter 5

"Trust me," Chrissy whispered to Caroline as they tiptoed around the edge of the Golden Gate Park rose garden.

"This is crazy." Caroline sighed. "Ouch!" She pulled a rose branch off her arm. "Isn't there a better way to get into the movies?"

"In show business, if you want to get ahead, you need contacts, right?"

"I guess."

"So trust me. I told you, Cara, they're filming a scene here for *Denim Blues,* and we're going to be extras. If everything works out like I planned, we'll be signing on the dotted line before sunset to be stars." Chrissy motioned Caroline to get down on her knees and follow her through a lush tunnel of roses.

"I am not crawling through there, Chrissy. I can't believe I let you talk me into this. I guess I was so excited yesterday, I'd have agreed to anything." Caroline stood up straight and placed her hands on her hips as a rose bush brushed her head. "Ouch!" she repeated. "Where exactly are we going anyway? You haven't even said yet."

"To the Japanese tea garden," Chrissy answered.

"Then why don't we walk over to the entrance and go in?" Caroline untangled her nubby-knit sweater from a thorny branch. "I'll even pay your dollar admission charge. Anything to get out of this jungle."

Chrissy sat down in the dirt and turned to Caroline. "We can't go in the entrance. They might see us."

"But I thought you said you'd seen a notice for extras to show up here today," Caroline said. "Don't we want them to see us?"

"Not yet," Chrissy replied, crawling back out of the tunnel.

"Why not?" Caroline asked in a threatening voice.

Chrissy stood up and pretended to be admiring the roses. "Because the notice I saw was on Adam's clipboard, and it wasn't exactly a public announcement asking for extras. It was just a schedule for filming that I happened to catch a glimpse of."

Caroline glared at her cousin. Then, without a word, she stomped off across the park.

Chrissy ran to catch up with her. "Look, Cara, I'm sorry I wasn't completely straight with you when I asked you to come with me, but I knew you wouldn't come otherwise."

"That's right, Chrissy, I wouldn't have. I do want a part in the movie, but I don't think either of us will get one this way," Caroline declared.

"Why not?" Chrissy asked indignantly. "I read this article in *Teen Star* about how to break into the business, and it said that it was very important to make a lasting impression on the right people. And remember what Mr. Hayes said at the assembly about wanting girls who were creative and energetic for these parts? Besides, I'm Shannon, so I'm supposed to be a nonconformist."

"All right, all right. Our chances are so slim anyway, it can't hurt," Caroline said, turning to Chrissy. "We'll go to the tea garden, but not through those rosebushes. I know a back entrance that I've seen the gardeners use."

Ten minutes later, the girls were gazing at a movie feast for the eyes. They were still a good distance away, but close enough to see the film equipment set up around the pagoda. Cameras, microphones, and lights seemed tangled up in miles of thick cable. Chrissy recognized Justin pacing wildly and flailing his arms in disgust, but she couldn't hear what he was saying. She didn't see Adam or Josh anywhere. To the right just beyond the high curved bridge, she noticed a row of trailers. *That must be where the guys stay in between takes,* she thought. Just then Caroline pointed to Pete and Nick, sitting beneath a yellow awning at a makeshift makeup station located on the other side.

Poor Nick, Chrissy thought. While she couldn't see his expression, she could see a woman showering his dark curls with hair spray. She was obviously trying to make his hair stand up straight, but it kept springing back into its natural wave.

"Look at that woman slobbering all over Nick," Chrissy snarled.

"She's not half as bad as that one with the powder puff," Caroline added, motioning toward the woman hovering over Pete. "Hey! Look! Everyone is moving in this direction. I think they're going to film something."

Suddenly, the lights around the center pool and the giant Buddha became brighter, blinding the girls with a fierce glare.

"Let's go over there," Chrissy suggested, squinting her eyes and pointing to the giant Buddha. "I'll bet we can watch them shoot the whole scene from there." She darted over to the bonsai tree, around the goldfish pond, and up the back side of the giant Buddha. Reluctantly, Caroline tagged along only a few paces behind.

"Quiet! Quiet on the set!" Justin Hayes called out. The noise level on the set went immediately from a dull roar to complete silence.

"What power!" Chrissy whispered to Caroline.

"No kidding," Caroline replied softly. Then her voice rose, as the excitement of the moment seemed to overwhelm her. "Look, here come Pete and Nick!"

"Where? I can't see them." Chrissy craned her neck to get a better view.

"You'd better stay down and keep still," Caroline warned, pulling her cousin by the shirt.

"Do you see any extras?" Chrissy asked.

"Nope. Just the guys," Caroline answered. She gave her cousin a suspicious look. "I thought you said they were using lots of extras today. We can't exactly go out there and be extras if they don't need any."

"I don't understand. I'm sure the schedule said they'd be filming a crowd scene this afternoon." Chrissy slid down to the base of the statue and leaned her back against the cool stone.

"You've had some stupid ideas before, Chrissy, but this one—"

"Action!" The loud voice of Mr. Hayes interrupted Caroline's lecture. "Give me all you got, men, this is a take," he continued.

Chrissy and Caroline froze like statues. For a moment they didn't even dare breathe. But the dialogue was so faint that Chrissy could barely understand the conversation, let alone see what was going on. She edged her way slowly to the elbow of the Buddha's arm. Cautiously, she peered around his side to get a better look.

Holy mazoley! Chrissy thought. *Is he ever gorgeous!* Nick was standing only about eight feet away. He was in the middle of an intense argument with Pete. He grabbed Pete by his jacket and hurled him against the side of the Japanese bridge.

"What's going on?" Caroline mouthed to Chrissy.

Chrissy leaned out just far enough to hear Pete tell Nick where his sister, Julie, was hiding.

"Now what about the money you owe me?" Pete demanded.

"Nick owes Pete some money, but he doesn't have it to pay back right now, and besides, he says Pete's not good enough for his sister," Chrissy relayed.

"What?" Caroline strained to hear. "I can't see anything on this side. Trade with me, please?"

"No way," Chrissy replied, waving Caroline away. "They're just getting to the good stuff."

"How would I know?" Caroline mumbled.

"Quit complaining!" Chrissy hissed. "Just shimmy yourself closer to the Buddha's elbow and stand on the base. Hurry! They're about to sit on the bridge railing."

Quickly, Caroline maneuvered herself onto the base of the statue, as Chrissy had instructed. Chrissy breathed a sigh of relief and turned her attention back to the scene in front of her.

"You had no right to interfere in my family's business," Nick said, slicking back his hair.

"Yeah . . . well, if you would pay a little more attention to your sister and stop hanging out with that Shannon for a change, you might not be in this situation."

Shannon! That's me! Chrissy thought, inching out farther.

"Practice what you preach, buddy," Nick snapped. "I don't see you giving up any dates with Julie to spend time at home."

"Hey, Caroline!" Chrissy whispered loudly. "He's talking about you."

"I heard, I heard," Caroline answered. "This is great!"

By now the girls had nearly forgotten that they were on a film set. Nick and Pete were only a few feet away, and that was all that mattered. Chrissy's head poked out from behind the statue, in full view of the camera, and Caroline had hooked her arm around the front of the statue to get a better grip.

"What a terrific head start to help us develop our characters," Caroline remarked.

"I wonder if this scene is happening before or after my big scene with Nick," Chrissy replied, glancing down at her cousin. When she looked back up, she noticed that Nick and Pete had stopped arguing and were staring in her direction with amused grins on their faces. Everyone else on the set was staring as well, but, unfortunately, no one else was grinning.

"Cut!" Mr. Hayes screamed at the top of his lungs. "What in heaven's name is going on over there?"

For the second time, Chrissy and Caroline

froze. Every muscle in Chrissy's body went stiff. *Maybe if I don't move, he'll think I'm another statue,* she thought.

"You, miss, and you, young lady, what do you think you're doing on the set while we're filming?"

As each word roared out of his mouth, Mr. Hayes's voice increased in volume.

"Come here, please," he said, enunciating every syllable as he paced back and forth like a lion in a cage.

The girls looked at each other. Chrissy bit her bottom lip and moved slowly away from her perch, while Caroline eased down from the base of the Buddha. Caroline followed Chrissy as they sidestepped their way toward the director.

"Maybe it won't be so bad," Chrissy whispered.

"Sure, that's what Joan of Arc said before she became French toast."

"What are you girls doing here?" Mr. Hayes asked sternly. "We are trying to work. This is a business. Every wasted minute costs us money." His voice was now back up to full volume, and Chrissy wished she could melt into the pavement. "Take five!" he shouted. "Better make it ten. We'll need the extra time to escort these ladies out of here."

"I'm sorry, Mr. Hayes," Chrissy blurted out. "We thought we were supposed to be extras in the film this afternoon."

"As you can see, there are no extras here," he said sullenly. "We rewrote the scene the other night specifically so that we wouldn't need extras."

"Sorry," Chrissy said with a shrug. "Not even that group over there?" Chrissy pointed to three men and two women standing by the director's chair.

"That group, young lady, are the producers of this film. So if it's not too much trouble, Miss . . . uh?"

"Chrissy," she answered energetically. "Chrissy Madden."

She knew that Mr. Hayes was trying to exert his power over her—and at first she had to admit he'd succeeded. But then she told herself that at least she'd made a lasting impression, and she decided to use that to her advantage.

Obviously, he had succeeded entirely with Caroline, however. "Let's just go, Chrissy," she pleaded, tugging on Chrissy's T-shirt and backing up.

"I've seen you somewhere before, haven't I, Miss Madden?"

"Yes, sir, Mr. Hayes," Chrissy replied, rocking proudly on her heels. "I passed . . . well, actually"—she pulled Caroline back to her side—"we both got to fill out green cards at the casting call yesterday. So we get to try out with Pete and Nick on Saturday." She beamed at the director.

"Fine," Mr. Hayes said with a sigh. He crossed to Chrissy and Caroline and put his arms around the girls' shoulders. "I'll see you then," he continued coolly. He paused for a moment, then suddenly changed his tone. "On second thought, as long as you're here, you might as well see the scene filmed correctly," he said graciously. "Granted, you won't be as close to the action as you were a few minutes ago, but you might be able to hear and see a little better." He still had an edge to his voice, but at least he wasn't yelling, Chrissy thought.

"Do you think we could meet Pete and Nick, too?" she asked impulsively.

"Chrissy!" Caroline hissed.

"I don't think that's such a good idea," Mr. Hayes said. "You two are very attractive girls, and Pete and Nick need to concentrate so we can finish the scene before sundown." He smirked, then motioned to a pair of director's chairs arranged beneath the shade of a tree. "You should be comfortable over here," he continued. He'd opened his mouth to say something else, when Josh and Adam approached from behind the girls.

"We've got this morning's rushes back from the lab," Adam began. Then both he and Josh stopped short in surprise when they saw who was with their boss.

Mr. Hayes looked relieved to see them. "Glad you're here, boys. Why don't you get the ladies whatever they need—except our stars, of course," Mr. Hayes added jokingly. "Now, I have a film to make." He shifted gears and snapped his crew into action. "Let's get back to work."

"So we meet again," Adam said, pulling his

chair closer to Caroline's. "I didn't think I'd see you again so soon."

"Me either," Caroline answered, sitting down. "I can't believe I let Chrissy talk me into this. There must be a part of me that actually wants to do these crazy things, or else I wouldn't go along with it all the time. Boy, I sure do get stuck a lot." She shook her head in embarrassment.

Gently, Adam placed his hand on Caroline's arm, and Chrissy noticed her cousin smile and relax.

I'm glad they're getting along so well, she thought. *Adam seems really nice, and after all, it has been awhile since Cara has heard from Luke. In a way it's too bad. Cara and Luke seemed like a fairy-tale couple—sophisticated girl from San Francisco falls in love with farm boy from Iowa. Well, maybe now I'll have to change that to a college boy from Berkeley,* she thought, turning her own attention to Josh, whom she still thought looked like a Greek god. He'd just finished having a quiet word with Mr. Hayes, and had pulled up a chair next to hers.

"Do you think I made a lasting impression?" Chrissy asked him.

"Well, let's just say you definitely made an impression," he answered with a grin. "There's nothing you can do about it now."

Chrissy sighed. "That bad?"

"Let me put it another way. I don't think Justin will forget you," he said, running a hand through his blond hair. "Darn! Adam, we forgot to mark the film cans from this morning's rushes."

Adam put a hand up to his forehead. "You're right. Excuse us, girls. We'll be right back."

Chrissy nodded, her mind reeling. She'd got Mr. Hayes to notice her now, but how could she change his bad impression to a good one?

"Earth to Chrissy," Caroline called out. "You've got that scrunched-up look on your face again, and that usually means you're up to something, so stop. You've done enough damage for one afternoon."

"You didn't seem to mind so much when Adam was here," Chrissy teased, settling herself back into the chair.

"Adam has nothing to do with it," Caroline protested.

"But you do like him, don't you?" Chrissy asked eagerly.

"Just as much as you like Josh. I saw you gawking at him."

"Quiet! Quiet on the set, please!" Justin shouted as he glared at the twosome. "We're going to try this again, and this time let's have no interruptions." He shot the girls another look that could have melted stone. Chrissy straightened up and crossed her legs, then held her head up high, smiled politely, and gave Justin a respectful nod of approval. Caroline, on the other hand, slumped lower in her chair.

Josh and Adam returned to their posts next to the girls, and they all waited for Pete and Nick to make their entrance.

"Isn't this exciting?" Chrissy whispered. "I can't wait until it's our turn to be in front of the camera."

Just then Pete and Nick sauntered out of their trailers, and once again Chrissy was under the spell of movie magic.

The actors repeated the scene they had just done, but this time it was even better. Chrissy was in awe at the ease with which the whole process evolved, and the skill of everyone involved, from the key grip to Nick Matthews.

Besides being gorgeous, he was a wonderful actor, she thought. *I wish I could do it as effortlessly as he does. I just know we'd make a great team.*

"Cut and put it in the can," Justin called, leaping out of his chair. "That was perfect, everyone. Great job, fellas. You can take a break while we set up the next shot."

The guys gave each other a high-five slap, then headed toward their trailers. Chrissy tugged on Josh's jacket sleeve. "Since you're Nick's bodyguard, do you think you could introduce us?"

"Chrissy, you ask too much," Caroline scolded.

"It's all right, Chrissy," Josh teased. "I'll see if the guys have set up any interviews or plan to work out. I'm sure they won't mind a short introduction."

"Thanks, Josh," Chrissy said, her blue eyes glowing with excitement.

"How does my hair look?" she asked Caroline

as Josh took off across the grass toward the trailers.

"Fine, Chrissy," her cousin answered abruptly.

"I wish I hadn't worn these jeans," Chrissy complained, looking down at her waist. "They make me look fat."

Adam shook his head in amusement. "Chrissy, I don't know what you're worried about. Nick is a regular person, just like the rest of us."

"It's all set," Josh said, returning to the group.

"Holy cow!" Chrissy squealed. "I can't believe we're going to meet them today!" Chrissy said, spinning around.

"We can't wait all day," Josh said, sitting in Chrissy's chair. "They will have to go back to work before the week is over," he said with a twinkle in his eye.

Chrissy sucked in her stomach. "Okay, I'm ready."

"Good. Come on, gang."

Chrissy glanced over at Caroline as they followed Josh across the lawn, and she smiled to herself when she found her cousin pulling out a small tube of lip gloss from her pocket.

"They're both in Pete's trailer. Nick's using his Gravity Boots and Pete's signing pictures," Josh said. "You can only stay a few minutes. I don't think Justin would appreciate this."

"Okay," Chrissy promised, taking a deep breath to calm her nerves.

Josh pushed open the door of Pete's trailer. The small interior was cool and calming, and the deep brown carpet squashed under Chrissy's feet. She was surprised to see one long wall of shelves filled with books. Caroline had obviously seen the books, too, for her eyes lit up like fireworks. In the corner, Chrissy noticed the silhouetted figure of Pete Becker signing autographs. Then she spied Nick hanging upside down from the Gravity Boots at the end of the hall.

"Hi," he said. "You must be Chrissy."

Chapter 6

"How did you know me?" Chrissy asked as she took a step forward and looked down at Nick's face. Even upside down he was the best-looking guy she'd ever seen. She was so enraptured, she barely even noticed Caroline and Pete slip out the door.

"I understand you want to be an actress," he said.

"Oh, yes!" she exclaimed, moving a little closer.

"Actually, it's pretty boring. You end up doing a lot of just hanging around."

"Like what you're doing now," Chrissy said, indicating his unusual position.

"Exactly, but I guess it's got its good side, too."

"Like traveling, driving fast cars, wearing the coolest clothes, and eating in fancy restaurants?" Chrissy asked. *Darn! What a dumb thing to say,* she thought. *He must think I'm a real dork.*

"Yeah, that's just what it's like," Nick answered nonchalantly. "Look, why don't you take a seat?"

Chrissy's heart was pounding. She clasped her clammy palms together and sat down cross-legged on the floor facing Nick. *He looks so ordinary,* she thought suddenly, *hanging upside down like a monkey. He doesn't look like a movie star at all, just a guy hanging from his ankles.* It didn't seem so hard to imagine someone like him doing everyday chores like buying groceries or taking out the garbage. Somehow, this thought made him even more appealing to Chrissy, and a new, mature calm swept over her like an Iowa sunset.

"What was it like growing up in New York City?" she asked curiously.

"I didn't," Nick answered flatly.

"But *Teen Star* magazine said—"

"Do you believe everything you read?" Nick countered, his dark brown eyes studying her closely.

"I just figured it was all true." Chrissy's voice rang with disappointment.

"That's all right, it's part of the movies. Tell you what," he said gently, touching Chrissy's cheek," you can ask me anything . . . well, almost anything you want, and I'll give a straight answer."

"Okay," Chrissy replied in a daze. She could still

feel his touch on her face, and her mind flooded with a thousand thoughts. "So where did you grow up?"

"New Jersey. I did spend a lot of time in New York City, but I hate it when people think the two places are practically the same."

Chrissy nodded. "Yeah, I'd probably feel the same," she said. "Do you have any brothers or sisters?"

"Do I ever!" Nick said, laughing. "We have six kids in our family."

"Wow! I've got three brothers and they drive me crazy. I can't imagine six kids. You must live in a huge mansion." Chrissy's excitement grew and she pulled her knees to her chest and rested her chin on top.

"Don't you believe it, sunshine," Nick said, lightly mussing Chrissy's hair. "We lived in a tiny walk-up apartment until I started acting. Not exactly glamorous."

Chrissy was quiet for a moment. "How did you get into acting?" she asked. "You're really good."

"Thanks," Nick said, obviously pleased by the compliment. "To make a long story short, I used to spend my spare time acting with a local theater company. One night when we were doing *West Side Story*, this woman who used to come to all our productions brought her aunt with her. Well, this aunt had a friend who had a friend who had a brother-in-law who was an agent. And it's been nonstop ever since."

"Wow! That sounds like the plot of a movie," Chrissy remarked.

"So how about you?" Nick asked eagerly. "Tell me something about your life."

Chrissy thought for a moment. "Well, I'm a senior at Maxwell High. . . . "

She didn't even have a chance to mention Iowa, when Nick interrupted. "What are your plans for after you graduate?"

"Well, I'm really not sure yet," she said slowly. "I've been thinking about college, but now I think maybe I should just skip it and jump right into acting, like you."

"Go to school," Nick advised firmly. "If you want to get into acting, then major in it at college."

"But what difference would it make to my career? You made it big without going to college," Chrissy said.

Nick shook his head impatiently. "Chrissy, maybe college won't make a huge difference to your career, but believe me, it will make a huge difference to you as a person." He looked at her with serious eyes. "I'd love to be at college right now," he continued, "but my agent says that if I leave the business for four years to get a degree, my career will be down the drain. I guess I'm afraid to risk it. I wish I'd had the money to go to college a couple of years ago when I was right out of high school," he said wistfully. "Not that I'm unhappy now. It's just that I think everyone should have a chance to go on to college."

Chrissy didn't know what to say. He'd certainly given her a good argument for going to college.

"Hey, look, I'm sorry." Nick's face brightened and he smiled at Chrissy. "I didn't mean to lecture you. I guess all the blood has settled in my brain. I'd better get out of these boots."

"Can I ask one more question?" Chrissy asked, standing up and stretching her legs.

"Shoot." Nick turned himself right-side up.

Chrissy paused a moment to gather her courage. "Do you have a girl friend?" she asked shyly.

Nick shrugged. "Haven't got the time, sunshine," he answered. "Look, I gotta clean up before the next take, so I guess you'd better go." He rolled a towel around his shoulders and wiped the sweat from his brow. "I really enjoyed your visit. Maybe I can see you again while I'm in San Francisco," he suggested.

"Definitely," Chrissy said quickly. "I'll see you at the auditions."

"Right," Nick replied with a smile. Then he winked at Chrissy as she left the trailer.

Outside, she remained motionless for a moment, reliving the past twenty minutes. Her crazy stunt, as Caroline called it, had paid off better than she had ever imagined. She was determined, now more than ever, that she would get the part of Shannon. Back in the trailer, she and Nick had developed a special rapport, and Chrissy was sure that it would carry over to the screen. And perhaps if she acted the role of his girl friend on the screen, it would carry over into real life. *I've just got to find the perfect way to get this role*, she thought. *But in the meantime, I'd better find out how Cara's getting along.*

Chrissy was wandering down the hill toward the pagoda, when she caught sight of Caroline and Pete standing together on the Japanese bridge. They were obviously deep in conversation. Caroline and Pete? she thought, though she didn't know why she should be so surprised. Her cousin was very pretty and extremely intelligent—but somehow Chrissy had never imagined her with what Caroline herself had called "a teenybopper heartthrob." And what about Adam? Where were he and Josh, anyway?

As she creeped up closer to the bridge, Chrissy overheard pieces of Caroline's conversation with Pete, and she had to smile. Only Cara would talk to a gorgeous movie star about his collection of books!

"You like F. Scott Fitzgerald, too?" she was saying. "I think his work is terrific—so powerful."

Pete nodded. "I agree. *The Great Gatsby* especially gets to me every time I read it."

Chrissy couldn't hear her cousin's reply, but she nearly fell over when she heard Pete say, "You know, I'm glad you're taking acting lessons, Caroline. Maybe one day we could do a remake of *The Great Gatsby* together. You'd make a fantastic Daisy." He paused. "No, on second thought, you're a lot nicer than Daisy was."

Caroline smiled and blushed at the compliment, but before she could say anything, Justin's booming voice echoed throughout the gardens.

"Everybody on the set in five minutes!"

Pete's face fell. "Back to work. I wouldn't mind so much, except that Justin's timing is so darned bad."

"That's okay, I understand," Caroline assured him as they turned back toward the pagoda.

Panicking, Chrissy looked around for someplace to hide. The last thing she wanted was for Caroline to think she'd been eavesdropping. She needn't have worried. Caroline and Pete were so involved in their discussion that they didn't even notice her until they had nearly walked straight into her.

"Hi, Chrissy," Caroline greeted her cousin cheerfully. "You've met Pete, haven't you?"

Pete put out his hand to shake hers. "I saw you walk into the trailer with Cara before, but we haven't been properly introduced. I'm Pete Becker."

"I know," Chrissy said, grinning. Didn't Pete realize that nearly every girl in the whole country knew who he was? But from the way he was looking at Caroline, it seemed he had only one girl on his mind. *Amazing*, Chrissy thought. *I admit I go ga-ga over guys all the time, but Cara's different. At least she used to be, but this afternoon she's got Pete and Adam falling at her feet. And she sure looks like she's having fun!*

Chrissy was still marveling at the incredible change in her cousin when Josh ran over to the group.

"Here you are," he said, stopping to catch his breath. "I just went up to the trailers to look for you. Pete, you're wanted in costuming on the double."

"Right," Pete said. "See you later." With a meaningful look directed at Caroline, he took off over the bridge.

Josh sighed. "Do you know it took us all morning to arrange a location for a thirty-second scene that we're supposed to shoot tomorrow? But Justin has just decided he doesn't like it anymore. So he sent Adam out to find someplace else." He shook his head in sympathy. "Hey, girls, I nearly forgot. Nick asked if you wanted to watch him get made up. Vicki is giving him a black eye."

"Huh?" Chrissy asked, confused.

"She's making him up to look like he has a black eye," Josh explained. "Remember in the scene we just filmed, Nick and Pete had a fight?"

Chrissy and Caroline nodded.

"But it didn't look like anything serious," Caroline remarked. "Just a few light punches."

Josh grinned. "Ah, but that's the magic of movies. Just wait until the scene is edited and sound effects are dubbed in. Then you'll see."

"Well, what are we waiting for?" Chrissy asked. "I want to see Nick's bruiser."

Without another word, Josh led the girls across the bridge and quietly past Mr. Hayes, who was barking orders at a technician, to the makeup station.

"Listen, do me a favor and stay out of Vicki's way while she's working. She can be a real witch sometimes," Josh warned in a low voice as they approached the yellow awning covering the makeup station. "You girls go on in. I'm going to see if I can help Adam," he said, leaving the girls on their own.

The first thing Chrissy saw when she walked under the awning were Nick's chocolate-brown eyes gazing at her from a face covered with green slime. His hair was slicked back away from his face and he wore a towel wrapped around his neck like a bib.

"Hi, Chrissy," he greeted her, smiling to reveal his even white teeth.

The woman standing behind Nick's chair bristled. "Nick, darling, please shut your mouth. If you don't let me take this cold cream off your face right now, I'm afraid it will have to stay there permanently."

Giving Chrissy a sheepish look, Nick closed his mouth.

Even with green slime on his face he's gorgeous, Chrissy thought as she watched Vicki remove the cold cream with a tissue. She wanted to ask what the cream was for, but she didn't dare say a word. Luckily, Vicki suddenly started to enjoy having an audience.

"In case you're wondering," she began, pushing a strand of unruly red hair out of her eyes, "this cold cream is for cleansing, so Nick's face will be free of dirt when I put the makeup on."

Tentatively, Caroline walked forward to take a closer look. "But what's in it that makes it green?" she asked.

"Cucumbers," Vicki answered. "Best thing for combination skin." She finished removing the cream, then reached over to open a large metal box on the counter. It reminded Chrissy of the box her father used to carry his fishing tackle.

"What's in there?" she ventured.

Vicki slid the box across the counter to Chrissy. "See for yourself."

Peering into the box, Chrissy found several small containers of various hues, along with makeup pencils, brushes, a sponge, and a powder puff.

"We could put on a new face every day with this stuff," Caroline whispered, looking over her cousin's shoulder.

Chrissy gazed into the box, then over at Nick. "How are you going to do the black eye?" she asked Vicki.

"Well," Vicki began, "it's done with a combination of shading and color. What colors do you usually see in a black eye?" she asked.

Why, Vicki sounds as if she's teaching a lesson to a bunch of five-year-olds! Chrissy thought. *But as long as she doesn't mind our being here, I guess it doesn't matter.*

"A black eye is usually black and blue," she answered.

"And red and purple," Caroline chimed in.

"You're both right," Vicki told them, "but it

depends on how bad the bruise is, where he was hit, and sometimes with what object."

"I was hit in the eye with Pete's fist, so you can bet it's serious," Nick joked.

Vicki gave him an irritated glance. She obviously took her work very seriously. "First I check today's shooting schedule to find that the bruise is only about twelve hours old. That puts it in full bloom. The black, blue, purple, and red eye is the one we'll create. Since it was caused by Pete's hand, it will be fairly localized."

She pulled her makeup box back toward her and began rummaging through her supplies.

"For our bruise, we mix specific colors. The purple and blue tones go on the fleshy areas, and the red on the bony places."

As she spoke, Vicki blended the colors on Nick's face like an artist painting on a canvas. Chrissy watched in amazement as a realistic-looking wound appeared around Nick's eye. Taking a dab of grease paint, Vicki meticulously placed white dots around the edge of the bruise, then carefully blended the greasepaint toward the center.

"Wow!" Chrissy exclaimed. "It makes the whole eye look swollen."

"Precisely," Vicki said, stepping back to evaluate her finished piece.

"That's really amazing," Chrissy said, moving in for a closer look. She reached out to touch the corner of Nick's eye, when Vicki slapped it away quickly.

"Don't ever touch makeup before it's powdered," she snapped. With an angry glare at Chrissy, she proceeded to cover Nick's face in a translucent powder. "You girls shouldn't really be here anyway," she added.

"I asked them if they wanted to watch," Nick said, quickly closing his mouth just in time to receive a pat with the powder puff.

"Yes, that's right," Chrissy began, an idea forming in her head. "You see, Nick had told us what an expert makeup artist you are, so we came up with this idea of raffling off one of your professional makeovers to raise money for this scholarship fund we're setting up at school. And I can see by the terrific way you did his black eye that all the girls would be standing in line to have one of your makeovers." She stopped talking long enough to notice Caroline and Nick staring curiously at her. "Well, what do you say?" she asked Vicki.

Vicki smiled from ear to ear. "Well, I'd love to do it, but I just don't think I'll have the time while we're shooting *Denim Blues*." She glanced at her watch. "I have a few minutes now, though. Why don't I give you two some quick pointers so you can do the makeovers yourselves?"

"That'd be great!" Chrissy replied with relief. When she'd blurted out her idea, she hadn't known what to expect, but the more she thought about it, the more determined she became to set up the scholarship fund.

"Is my black eye finished, then?" Nick asked Vicki.

"Yup. You can go," she said, waving him away.

He got up and unwrapped the towel from around his neck, then headed out into the bright sunlight, motioning for Chrissy to follow him.

"What's all this about a scholarship fund?" he asked. "Why didn't you mention it before?"

Chrissy shrugged. "Because I just thought of it. I decided you were right when you said that everyone should have a chance to go on to college. The idea for the scholarship fund just popped into my head a minute ago."

"Well, it's a terrific idea," Nick said, giving her an admiring smile. "If there's anything I can do to help, just let me know."

"Actually, there is something," Chrissy began slowly. "Can you get some autographed pictures of you and Pete that we could auction off in a raffle? It would raise lots of money, and it's for a good cause. . . ."

Nick's smile grew wider and his brown eyes twinkled beneath his "wound." "No problem," he replied. "And I'll see what else Pete and I can scrounge up for you. Now, I'd better get down to the set—they can't start filming if their star spends all his time with a pretty blonde," he added with a wink of his "good" eye.

As Chrissy watched him make his way toward the pagoda with long, confident strides, she sighed contentedly. *Well, what do you know?* she thought, stepping back into the makeup station for her makeup lesson. *All my dreams are coming true!*

Chapter 7

"Is it true?" Tracy asked on Monday. "Did you really see them filming *Denim Blues* at the Japanese tea garden? And did you really get to talk to Nick Matthews and Pete Becker? And did you really—"

"Yes, it's all true," Chrissy interrupted. She slid into the seat next to Tracy as Caroline slid in next to Maria on the opposite side of the table at Mama's Ice Cream Store.

"Does your little adventure yesterday have anything to do with why you asked us all to meet here?" Maria asked.

Chrissy smiled mysteriously. "Sort of."

"Well, are you going to tell us what this is all about?" Maria prodded.

"I will," Chrissy replied, "when the others get here."

Tracy looked at her with mock irritation. "Well, do we have to wait to hear about what happened yesterday?" she asked. "I want to hear every single detail."

"Me, too," Maria chimed in.

Chrissy glanced across at her cousin. "Shall we tell them about it, Cara? Or should we keep them in suspense?"

"Let's keep them in suspense," Caroline replied with a mischievous grin.

"Keep who in suspense about what?" Randy asked as he squeezed in next to Chrissy.

"Hi, Randy," she greeted him. "Where's Justine? I thought she was coming with you."

"She said she'll be here as soon as she can. She put an outfit on hold at Macy's on Saturday, so she's gone back to get it," he explained.

"That's Justine," Maria remarked. "As if she didn't already have enough clothes. What's this outfit for?"

"That stupid audition next week. Sorry, I know you're all involved, too, but you haven't gone off the deep end like some people we know." Randy jerked his head in Maria's direction and crossed his arms over his chest.

"You're just jealous because Justine is paying more attention to Pete Becker than to you. What an ego," Maria joked.

"It's just a movie, for heaven's sake. You'd think

he'd asked her to marry him or something," Randy complained.

"There's always hope." Maria sighed.

"I even heard that two girls crashed the set yesterday afternoon," Randy went on. "Apparently they made complete fools of themselves in front of the whole crew."

Chrissy grinned proudly as Maria and Tracy exchanged glances and Caroline sank slowly into the booth.

"Hi, everybody," Justine called out cheerfully. "Wait until you see the new outfit I splurged on. It is the hottest. It cost me a month's allowance, but it'll be peanuts if I get cast in the film."

"I rest my case," Randy added, burying his head in his arms.

Justine set her shopping bag on the table and pulled out her new dress to a chorus of oh's and ah's from the others. At last Chrissy couldn't stand it any longer.

"I have something pretty hot to show you, too," she announced. She reached under the table for her book bag. "I know you guys are going to freak out when you see what I've got." Everyone watched as Chrissy carefully laid out a man's blue T-shirt, a pair of well-worn sneakers, and sunglasses.

"So?" Randy said. "I've got all these things at home, too."

Chrissy grinned mysteriously. "But these things are special," she declared.

"How?" Maria asked.

"Yeah. How?" Justine echoed. "I mean these sneakers must be at least a hundred years old."

Randy looked doubtfully at Chrissy. "Don't tell me these things are antiques."

"Nope," Chrissy replied, "much better than that. I got these things from—"

"Are you ready to order?" A waitress stood at the head of the table, order pad in hand.

Quickly everyone told her what they wanted. They'd all been to Mama's Ice Cream Store enough times to know the menu by heart.

"Where did you get this stuff from?" Maria asked when the waitress had gone.

Chrissy didn't answer. Instead, she turned over one of the sneakers so her friends could see what was written on the rubber sole:

Nick Matthews 10/11/87—left foot

"Nick Matthews?" Justine gasped. "This is . . . is Nick Matthews's sneaker?"

Chrissy nodded. "So's this one," she said, showing everyone the bottom of the other sneaker. "And the sunglasses are Nick's, too. That T-shirt is Pete's."

Tracy looked at her friend in awe. "No kidding. This stuff is for real?"

"You're not pulling a fast one on us, are you, Chrissy?" Maria asked.

"No, she's not kidding," Caroline answered for her cousin. "I wouldn't have believed it either, if I hadn't been there myself. When we were on the set of *Denim Blues* yesterday, we got to know Pete and Nick pretty well."

"You and Chrissy are the girls who crashed the set?" Randy asked. He shook his head in amazement.

"That's us," Chrissy said, grinning.

"So tell us what they're like," Justine begged. "Is Nick as nice as he looks?"

"Even nicer," Chrissy replied.

Randy rolled his eyes. "Do you girls talk like this about all guys?"

"Only movie stars," Maria answered.

Randy rolled his eyes again. "Well, just suppose I were a movie star. Would you say I'm as nice as I look?"

All the girls looked at one another with secretive smiles, as if they were holding a silent conference. At last Justine answered for all of them. "Yeah, you're even nicer than you look. In fact, you're even nicer than Nick's looks."

"Is that a compliment or an insult?" Randy asked. "I can't tell."

"I don't see what you're worried about, Randy. You know Justine only has eyes for you," Tracy said.

Justine put her hand on top of Randy's. "Tracy's right. You know you're the only one for me," she said quietly, giving him a quick kiss on the cheek.

"Ugh! That's enough, you two. No more mushy stuff," Maria objected. "Now, Chrissy, will you please tell us why you asked us to meet you here? Did you want to treat us all to some ice cream or something?"

"Wishful thinking," Tracy said with a grin.

Chrissy was about to defend herself when she noticed the waitress walking slowly toward their table balancing a tray of ice cream sundaes. Quickly Chrissy cleared the prized items from the table and stuffed them into her book bag. "Ice cream first, talk second," she said.

The waitress set down their sundaes and for a moment everyone was silent as they dug into their treats with gusto.

"Mmm," Chrissy said, sighing contentedly. "This hot fudge really hits the spot." She took another scoop and let the cool, creamy mixture melt in her mouth as she gazed around the table at her friends. "We are here because we are about to make Maxwell High history," she announced.

Four pairs of curious eyes looked at Chrissy.

"How?" Tracy asked.

"Chrissy's got this great idea," Caroline said enthusiastically. "Go on, Chrissy, tell them about it."

Chrissy swallowed another spoonful of ice cream. "Since coming to San Francisco, I've really opened up my eyes to different things, and one thing I've come to realize is how important it is to go on to college. My parents have been telling me that for years, but back in Danbury it didn't seem like such a big deal."

"I don't get it. What does college have to do

with making Maxwell High history?" Justine interrupted.

"And what does any of this have to do with Pete Becker and Nick Matthews?" Maria added.

"Well, when I was talking to Nick yesterday, he was saying that he really regrets not having had the chance to go to college," Chrissy explained patiently.

"But he got to be a big movie star anyway, so it didn't matter that he didn't go to college," Randy remarked.

Carefully, Chrissy placed her spoon on the table. "Nick doesn't see it that way. He says he's missing out—and the only reason is because his family couldn't afford to pay for college." She paused to take a deep breath. "So I was thinking about some kids at Maxwell who are really smart, but they're in the same position that Nick was in."

"Chrissy, get to the point," Caroline whispered. "Everybody's waiting to hear your idea."

"Okay," Chrissy agreed. She leaned forward in her seat and waited until she had everyone's undivided attention. "I propose that we start up a scholarship fund at Maxwell High," she said, glancing around the table to see her friends' reactions.

"That's a great idea, Chrissy, but we need money for a scholarship," Tracy reminded her.

"We'll raise the money," Chrissy replied. "That's what those goodies in my book bag are for. Nick and Pete gave that stuff to us so we could auction it off to benefit the scholarship fund."

"They gave us something else to auction off as well, but we can't let you see until we've all finished eating," Caroline added.

"What is it?" Maria asked.

"Autographed pictures." Caroline grinned and scooped up a spoonful of ice cream.

"Wow!" Tracy said in awe.

Justine's eyes lit up. "No kidding. I bet we'll raise a lot of money auctioning those off."

"So you'll do it, then?" Chrissy asked.

"I'm in," Tracy said without hesitating.

"Me, too."

"And me."

"Yeah, I'll do it, too."

"Stop looking at me like that, Chrissy," Caroline complained. "You know I'm all for it."

"Great!" Chrissy sat back in her seat wearing a pleased smile. *I'm finally proving to everyone that my ideas aren't always crazy,* she thought, dipping her spoon into the sundae dish. *It's nice to know that we're going to be helping someone, too. I think I really deserve this ice cream.*

Anticipating a spoonful of cold, refreshing mint chocolate-chip ice cream topped with hot fudge and whipped cream, Chrissy closed her eyes and opened her mouth. "Yuk!" she exclaimed, her bright smile changing to a wry expression as her eyes flew open.

"What's wrong?" Caroline asked her cousin.

"I guess I've been talking too much. Look at what happened to my sundae." Chrissy tipped her spoon over the dish and a greenish-brown liquid dribbled in.

"That looks absolutely disgusting," Maria said, laughing.

Tracy gave Chrissy a sympathetic look. "I'd offer you some of mine, but I ate it all."

"I've finished my sundae, too, but I'm still hungry," Randy remarked.

"You're always hungry," Justine told her boyfriend, as she reached over to pat his lean stomach. "Honestly, if he had the chance, he would eat every minute of the day," she added to the others.

"That's it," Chrissy said. "Justine, you and Randy came up with the perfect idea for another fund raiser."

"We did?" Randy asked.

"Everybody likes food, right?" Chrissy went on.

"Right," the others agreed.

"So we'll have a bake sale."

"Yeah," Maria agreed. "We can set up a table in the cafeteria and sell goodies during lunch."

"Everybody hates school lunches, so we'd definitely be a hit," Justine added.

"I hate to burst your bubble," Caroline interrupted, "but it's against the rules to sell food in the cafeteria."

"You can say that again," Randy joked. "They haven't sold anything I'd call food in there since I came to Maxwell." Everyone laughed and nodded their heads in agreement.

"Seriously," Caroline went on. "The administra-

tion says that the cafeteria is only for the selling
of school lunches. But if we sell baked goods in
the commons area outside the cafeteria, we
should be okay," she suggested.

"Sure. Everyone will buy something for dessert
on the way into the cafeteria," Chrissy said,
nodding her head as she visualized the crowd
that would mob the bake-sale table. "So when
shall we have the sale?"

"How about if we have the auction and the
bake sale on the same day?" Tracy suggested.
"That way we could have a big publicity splash
all over the school for one special day that would
kick off the fund-raising campaign."

"That's a good idea," Chrissy agreed.

"Friday would be the best day, because everyone is in a better frame of mind," Maria said. "We
proved that in a survey in psychology class."

"Good point, Maria," Caroline remarked, taking
a small notebook out of her purse. "I'll mention it
to Mr. O'Brien."

"If no one else wants the job, I thought Cara,
here, would be the best person to talk to Mr.
O'Brien about all this," Chrissy explained. "We
have to check everything with him before we go
any further."

Caroline nodded. "That's right, but I don't think
we'll have any trouble. I mean, we are doing this
for a good cause."

"Hey! I bet we could raise hundreds by charg-
ing admission to the set of *Denim Blues*," Randy
suggested. "I bet there are lots of kids at Maxwell

who are just as starstruck as you girls. Or have Nick Matthews and Pete Becker visit Maxwell again, and sell tickets to the assembly."

"Hey! That reminds me," Caroline said, "we haven't talked about the makeovers yet, Chrissy."

"That's right!" Chrissy exclaimed, snapping her fingers. "You guys, it was so cool—when we were on the set, we watched the makeup artist give Nick a black eye, and it really looked real. Cara and I thought that could be one of our fund raisers, too."

"What? Giving people black eyes?" Randy asked.

"No, silly—giving people makeovers," Chrissy corrected him. "After we watched her do Nick's eye, Vicki—that's the makeup artist—showed us some professional techniques, stuff you don't even see in fashion magazines."

Justine's eyes lit up. "Will you show me some of those techniques?" she asked.

Caroline grinned. "I think we've got our first customer, Chrissy."

Chrissy grinned back. "If this keeps up, we'll be able to give someone a scholarship that pays for all four years of his college career!"

Chapter 8

"I'm going to start the video in five minutes, Chrissy," Caroline called from the Kirbys' kitchen. "Dad's made popcorn and Mom's got a fresh box of Kleenex."

"Start without me," Chrissy called back from her desk in the bedroom. "I'm still counting the profits for the scholarship fund."

"You can't miss the beginning of *To Have and Have Not*," Caroline explained, poking her head into the room. "It's our Friday night classic. Missing the beginning would be like skipping the first few chapters of a novel."

"I'll be there in a minute, okay? But listen to these totals first. I think the scholarship fund is off to a great start!" Chrissy exclaimed, patting the bed for Caroline to sit down. "We sold Nick's left sneaker for fifteen dollars and his right one for twelve." She glanced up at her cousin. "That was a good idea to sell them separately, Cara. Anyway, we got seventeen for Nick's sunglasses, and Pete's T-shirt went for twenty. So"—she paused, checking her calculations—"that's sixty-four dollars."

"Hey! That's not bad," Caroline remarked with admiration.

"Plus the forty-five dollars we made raffling off those autographed pictures makes one hundred and nine," Chrissy continued. "Then there's the bake sale—Cara, your extra-fudgy brownies were especially popular. We got rid of all one hundred of them, so that's another twenty-three dollars and fifty cents—"

"But Chrissy . . ." Caroline interrupted. She leaned against the doorframe and folded her arms in front of her. "I thought we charged twenty-five cents each for the brownies."

Chrissy looked up from her calculations. "We did," she replied sheepishly. "I guess you're wondering why we didn't make the whole twenty-five dollars if we sold all one hundred brownies." Caroline nodded. "Well . . . uh . . . unfortunately, I had the shift with Tracy during the lunch hour and we gobbled up some of the profits."

Caroline rolled her eyes in mock exasperation. "I should have known."

"You can't blame us, Cara. Your brownies are absolutely irresistible," Chrissy said.

"Did anyone buy your apple pie?" Caroline asked.

"Mr. Turner bought it," Chrissy replied with a grin. "He said he likes his pies well done. You know, he's not such a bad guy, after all, Cara. He gave me the three dollars for the pie, then gave me ten dollars extra to put toward the scholarship fund."

"Well, that's certainly a change," Caroline commented. "Just last week math was your worst subject and you thought Mr. Turner was a real tyrant."

"I know," Chrissy said. "But somehow he's much nicer now that I've started putting some effort into trig class. And do you know what he said today? He said he's proud to have students willing to give their time and energy to such a good cause."

She leaned back in her chair and stretched the kinks out of her arms. It certainly was hard work raising money for the scholarship fund. Luckily, her idea had received a lot of support—from Mr. Turner and the school principal, Mr. O'Brien, as well as from the students at Maxwell. Chrissy was amazed at how her idea had taken off, and she knew Nick would be pleased.

While she hadn't been near the film set since the previous weekend, Chrissy still thought about Nick all the time. It was only eight days until the auditions, and she was determined to get the part of Shannon. Then she could be with him as much as possible. And once she got the part, she could donate her beat-up old sneakers to be auctioned off for the scholarship fund.

"So far, I'm very impressed," Caroline said. "What about our makeovers? How much money did we make on those? I showed quite a few girls how to do up their faces like Vicki showed us, and they were really happy with the results. Dolores Wright said she looked even more stunning than usual after I did her face."

Chrissy avoided her cousin's gaze and put her paper and pencil down on the desk. She didn't have to look at her calculations to know how little they'd made on the makeovers. "So, are we ready for the movie?" she asked, purposely changing the subject.

"First tell me how much money we raised doing the makeovers," Caroline replied, giving her cousin a suspicious stare.

Glancing back at her calculations, Chrissy pretended to figure it out. "Ten dollars and fifty cents," she answered.

"That's not bad at all—I mean, we only charged fifty cents for a complete facial makeover, so that's a pretty good profit," Caroline said.

Chrissy didn't say anything.

"That is the profit, isn't it?" Caroline asked.

Chrissy shook her head. "That's how much we made on the makeovers, but the supplies cost eleven dollars and forty-nine cents, so we actually lost ninety-nine cents."

"But I must have made up at least twenty girls,"

Caroline protested. "How many did you do, Chrissy?"

"I made up a few that looked really nice— honest, they looked beautiful, Cara," she answered. "But then I started getting carried away and some of the girls wanted refunds. They said the makeovers might be more appropriate for Halloween."

Caroline walked over to Chrissy's chair with her hands on her hips and a menacing look on her face. Chrissy held her breath, waiting for the scolding from her cousin. Then suddenly a big grin spread across Caroline's face.

"Chrissy," she said, "what are we going to do with you?"

Chrissy shrugged. "Get me a part in the movie?"

"I'll tell you what—after we watch this video, maybe we can work on memorizing our scripts for *Denim Blues*," Caroline suggested. "Now hurry up!"

"Scripts?" Chrissy muttered after Caroline had left the room. "I haven't even looked at the script!" Panic started to set in and Chrissy dumped her book bag out on the bed, looking for the packet she'd received at the casting call. She'd been looking at her audition information whenever she had a chance, but somehow she hadn't read through the script more than a few times. Now she flipped open the envelope and stared blankly at the mass of typed pages of dialogue. *I'll never get all these lines memorized now,* she thought. *I should have started learning them ages ago.* She glanced briefly at each page, but shoved everything back into the envelope when she heard the M-G-M lion's roar from the living room.

"It's starting, Chrissy." Aunt Edith's voice rang down the hall. Chrissy slipped hurriedly into her fuzzy slippers and headed into the living room.

"I sure wish they made movies like that these days," Uncle Richard remarked over Saturday morning's breakfast.

"Lauren Bacall was just beautiful," Aunt Edith agreed. "You know, girls, she was just a year older than you two when she made that film."

"You're kidding!" Chrissy said in astonishment.

"I think she was very mature-looking for her age," Aunt Edith continued, as she buttered her croissant.

"It's that low, sexy voice of hers," Uncle Richard added, sweeping Aunt Edith up into his arms and bending her backward into a low dip. Everyone laughed as Aunt Edith tried to hide her embarrassed blush.

"What did you think, Chrissy?" Caroline asked, pouring herself another glass of juice. "I'm so glad Charles suggested I see it. I've got to tell him that at acting class today."

Chrissy put down her spoon in surprise. "Who's Charles?"

"He's the acting coach Loretta recommended. When I told her about the auditions, she sug-

gested I have more intensive acting lessons with
Charles instead of staying in her beginners'
class," Caroline explained. "Charles was so right
about Lauren Bacall—she puts her whole self
into the part, just the way I want to do with the
part of Julie."

"You've certainly chosen a good role model,"
Uncle Richard remarked.

"So what did you think, Chrissy?" Caroline
repeated.

"I thought it was fine," Chrissy answered, scoot-
ing a raisin around the bottom of her cereal bowl.
In truth she'd thought the movie was just okay—
she much preferred modern movies to old black-
and-whites.

"Well," Aunt Edith said, "I'm off to the gallery.
I've got to set up that new exhibit today." She got
up and put her dishes in the sink, and Uncle
Richard followed with his.

Chrissy was just finishing the last of her cereal
when the telephone rang.

"Caroline, it's for you," Uncle Richard called
from the hallway.

"Must be Justine calling to talk about the
audition," Caroline said as she went to pick up
the phone.

What am I going to do about the audition?
Chrissy wondered, as she got up to stack the
dishes in the dishwasher. *Lauren Bacall just isn't
my style.*

"You'll never guess in a million years who that
was," Caroline squealed.

By the look on her cousin's face, Chrissy could tell it hadn't been Justine who'd called. It must have been . . .

"Pete Becker!" she exclaimed, dropping the spoons in the sink.

"Not quite," Caroline added, twirling around. "It was Adam. He just called to say that he's going to go through the film archives at Berkeley this afternoon to do research for one of his classes and wondered if we'd want to go with him. It sounds interesting, don't you think?"

More ancient movies, Chrissy thought. *No, thank you.* "You go ahead, Cara," she replied, "I still haven't looked at the script yet, and I have a little more trig to keep on top of. Besides, I think Adam would enjoy spending the afternoon alone with you."

"Are you sure?" Caroline asked. "He invited both of us, and I know he meant it."

"I'm sure he did," Chrissy said, pushing the kitchen chair under the table. "Tell him thanks just the same, but I think I'd better start getting ready for that audition—especially since we fell asleep last night before we got a chance to read over our lines. You don't mind, do you?"

"No, of course not." Caroline paused. Then her blue eyes lit up. "Hey! I've got the answer. Why don't you come with me to my acting session with Charles? After the class, you can decide whether you want to go to the archives. You did say you wanted some acting tips, and Charles is the best, so you might as well learn it from him."

Chrissy looked doubtful. "Oh, I don't know, Cara. I think I'm better off preparing for the audition on my own."

"How do you know?" Caroline asked. "Come on. One class won't hurt. Then if you like it, you can go for more."

"All right," Chrissy agreed. "I may as well give it a try."

"Great! Grab your dance gear and I'll call Adam and ask him to meet us at the studio this afternoon."

"Dance gear?" Chrissy echoed. "What do I need my leotard and tights for?"

"To keep your body fluid and free while you do the exercises."

"But I thought that this was acting, not ballet."

"It is, silly," Caroline said, laughing. "But we do exercises in acting class, too. It's all a part of becoming a true artist."

"Artist? You mean now we have to paint, too?" Chrissy teased. *I guess Caroline knows what's best*, she thought as she and Caroline headed to their room to gather their dance gear. "Which shoes will I need to take?" Chrissy asked Caroline. "Shall I take a pair of your ballet slippers, or just wear my sneakers?"

"It doesn't matter," Caroline answered. She placed her leotard and tights in the same bag that she had used for her years of dance lessons. "In class you don't wear shoes at all, so you can feel the karma of the wooden floors."

"Karma," Chrissy mumbled to herself. "I hope it's not contagious."

"Charles is the absolute best," Caroline explained. "I had a little trouble understanding his motives at first, but once you trust him and see the results, you'll love him as much as I do."

"If you say so," Chrissy said halfheartedly. *Caroline is as gung-ho about these acting classes as she used to be about ballet class,* she thought. *Well, I'm sure it will pay off. If Cara's as good at acting as she was at dancing, she's got a part for sure.*

Grabbing her script, just in case, Chrissy slipped on her jacket and tore out the door after her cousin to catch the bus to Telegraph Hill, where The Acting Studio was located.

"I'm really excited about you coming to class with me," Caroline reassured Chrissy. "I've never had a guest before. Charles is always encouraging his students to bring in visitors. He says it adds new energies to the aura, and when you do that, you can change into a completely new individual."

Chrissy smiled and tried to stay relaxed. Usually she was up for new adventures, but today she wasn't too sure about Charles transforming her into a new individual.

Chapter 9

"Caroline, hello," a small, wiry, balding man said, greeting her with a warm smile. "And I see you've brought a guest," he added, turning to Chrissy.

"This is my cousin, Chrissy," Caroline said by way of introduction. "Chrissy, this is Charles, the wonderful acting teacher I told you about."

"How do you do?" Chrissy said politely. She put her hand out and he shook it firmly.

When he finally let go, Charles looked closely at her. "You are a person with enormous amounts of energy," he said. "I can sense it."

"That's Chrissy," Caroline said. "See? I told you he was incredible."

"You will be an asset to our group," Charles continued as he led the girls down the narrow hallway to the locker room. "Change your clothes and we'll begin. It looks like a small group today, so I'll be able to give your electrifying cousin some special attention." He took his leave while the girls began to change.

"I really think he likes you," Caroline said, encouraged. "I just knew you two would hit it off."

"You think so?" Chrissy answered as she slid into her tights and leotard. "What kind of things can he tell us about getting into the movies? Has he ever worked with any famous people before?"

"Hundreds," Caroline answered. "When we go into the studio, look at all the autographed pictures he has framed on his walls. It's like a Who's Who of modern drama."

"Terrific," Chrissy replied. She pulled her blond hair back into a long ponytail and shuffled her feet along the carpet. "My feet are itching to catch the karma from the wooden floors in the studio."

"Chrissy, sometimes you can be so weird," Caroline remarked, giving her cousin a gentle push from behind. "Let's go to class."

When the girls entered the studio, Chrissy headed immediately for the wall to investigate the stars' photographs. She was certain none of them would be as cool as her own personally autographed pictures from Nick and Pete, but she figured it was the best way of checking out Charles's credentials.

"Not now," Caroline whispered, pulling Chrissy

away, "they've started without us."

In the center of the room, six people were lying down with their heads all meeting in the center of the circle like spokes of a wheel. A few people moved over to make space so Chrissy and Caroline could join in. At the center of the formation was Charles, giving commands in quiet, rhythmic order.

"Make sure that you are touching the hands and feet of the people on either side of you. You should also be able to feel the temporal plates of the skull of the person to the right and to the left of you."

Chrissy wasn't sure if her plates were touching anything, and since she wasn't positive what they were anyway, she went along with the crowd.

"We will begin with a few breathing exercises. As I count to eight, slowly raise your right arm until it is like an extension of your ears."

In an overexaggerated fashion, Charles demonstrated the exercise. Chrissy watched, then raised and lowered her arms and then her legs with the rest of the class.

"Breathe deeply with each count and feel the strength of the group's energy when you return to your original position."

This is great, Chrissy thought to herself as she coordinated with the rhythm of the other students. *I've been raising my arms and legs for years without knowing it could turn me into a new individual.*

"Now, on this final eight count, lift your head

slightly and then raise your limbs, so that every-thing but the trunk of your body is off the floor. We will hold that pose for twenty seconds, inhal-ing deeply. Gently tense your muscles while maintaining your balance. Ready, begin."

That's not hard, Chrissy thought, performing the exercise with ease. But at the final count, Chrissy felt like a turtle that had been set on its shell. She could feel a cramp developing in her right insole, and her back swayed back and forth. By the time Charles was commanding the stu-dents to release their tensions, Chrissy's body was so tense that no matter how hard she tried, she couldn't relax it. She reached up to soothe the shooting pain in her instep, but as she stretched her arm, her body rocked threaten-ingly from side to side, finally rolling over to land face down just inches away from Caroline.

"Chrissy!" Caroline cried. "What are you trying to do?"

"I got this cramp in my foot and lost my balance," she explained as she gently turned herself over to a sitting position.

"Please! Please!" Charles hollered. "We're go-ing to have to start again if we can't maintain our relaxed state. Now quietly get into pairs for our mirror-image exercise."

Caroline grabbed Chrissy's arm and led her over to a corner of the room.

"Just do everything I do, as if you were looking into a mirror," she instructed. The girls faced each other with their hands pressed together. As

Charles directed the class through various movements, Chrissy tried to imitate the exact way her cousin did them, even blinking at the same time as Caroline.

"I like this one," Chrissy remarked. "Maybe we could find a way to put this into our audition for *Denim Blues.*"

"Quiet, please," Charles ordered, giving Chrissy an impatient stare. "You must maintain total concentration to receive the full extent of the exercise. We'll do one more warm-up, and then I have a new experiment to try."

The next exercise they did was called The Machine. Chrissy liked this one even better than the mirror images. Caroline started The Machine by bending over at the waist and moving her arms in a circle in front of her, as if swimming the breaststroke. A boy joined the movement by bending from side to side in time with Caroline. One at a time, each pupil added his own movement to complete the big machine. Chrissy was the last one on, and she could hardly contain her creativity. Not only did she jog in place and wave her arms up and down like a bird, but she also clapped her hands on every fifth beat. When they finished the exercise, she was exhausted, but she couldn't refuse when Charles asked her to be his partner in the new experiment in honor of her being a guest in the class.

This is actually kind of fun now, Chrissy thought. *But what do all these exercises have to do with acting?* she wondered, turning her attention to Charles.

"We will begin this first segment by facing our partners and staring into their eyes," he instructed. "Use this time to look deeper than the superficial layers of skin and tissue. We will get to know the soul of the individual that faces us. Then we will delve into the exercise entitled No Exit."

He turned to stare into Chrissy's face with his watery blue eyes. He looked so serious that she wanted to laugh.

"Do you know you have freckles on your nose?" Chrissy asked, peering at Charles's face. "They're real tiny, but there sure are a lot of them."

"We're not interested in the features you can see with the eyes," Charles tried to explain as he shifted uncomfortably in his cross-legged pose.

"How else am I supposed to see if I don't use my eyes?" Chrissy asked.

"Look with your mind," Charles directed.

Beads of sweat had started appearing on his brow, and Chrissy could sense that he was losing his concentration. The other students stopped their own gazing to watch Chrissy and Charles. She hadn't meant to embarrass him, but she simply couldn't see the point to the exercise.

"I'm sorry," Chrissy apologized. "I didn't mean to ruin the exercise."

"You are not supposed to talk, Chrissy," Charles said, forcing a smile. His eyes wandered from

Chrissy's face to his other students, who were still watching with interest. "Okay, class, let's go on to the next exercise. In this one, two people stand in front of the class and pretend that they are in a room together. One person wants to leave the room, but the other one doesn't want to let him go. For example"—Charles took a deep breath, which seemed to give him confidence—"Chrissy and I are in a room." He motioned for her to join him in front and stand beside him. Determined not to mess up this time, Chrissy focused in on Charles's every word. "Now, how are you going to get out of the room?" he questioned.

"I'll open the door and walk out," she answered, confident that she'd arrived at the right answer.

"But the door is locked."

"Then I'll use a key," Chrissy replied.

"Your key doesn't fit the lock," Charles said, looking down on Chrissy with narrowed eyes.

"I'll call the locksmith to bring the right key." Chrissy placed her hands on her hips. *He's trying to trick me, but I'm not as dumb as he thinks,* she mused.

"The phones are out of order," Charles snapped back after a long pause.

"Then I'll break the door down with my body." Chrissy was beginning to get tired and angry at this game, and she wasn't too pleased with Charles either.

"The door is made of steel," he continued.

"Then I'll burn a hole in it with my blowtorch."

Chrissy had moved in close to Charles now and was practically freckled nose to freckled nose with him.

"Your torch has no fuel."

"Then I'll just walk out this way." Chrissy pivoted from the spot where she was standing and marched off the small platform where they had been acting out their scene.

"You can't do that," Charles commanded.

"Why not?" Chrissy asked. "You said the object of the game was to get out of the room, so I just walked out."

"But you can't break the fourth wall."

"I don't see any wall," Chrissy said.

At that, the class burst into laughter.

"The fourth wall means the space that faces the audience," Caroline explained. "You don't really see it, Chrissy."

Chrissy shook her head in exasperation. *Acting is just pretending you're someone else,* she reasoned, *so why all these exercises and this fourth-wall stuff? I don't think Charles can help me get the part of Shannon,* she decided.

She looked at the other students sitting on the floor in front of her—all except Caroline were whispering and giggling. She tried to catch her cousin's eye, but Caroline was staring down at the floor, an angry look on her face. *I bet she wishes she hadn't brought me here today,* Chrissy thought. *I guess I can't blame her.*

"I'm sorry for ruining your class, Charles," she

said as she turned to go. "I'll leave now before I cause any more trouble."

"That's all right," Charles growled. "Class is over now anyway." He gave Chrissy a ferocious glare, then walked out ahead of her into the hallway.

Without a word to Chrissy, Caroline stormed past and out the door, followed by the rest of the class, still whispering and giggling. "It's just a game," Caroline tried to explain, as Chrissy caught up with her.

"I know you like Charles, but I don't see how anything he's shown us is going to help us get into the movies," Chrissy said softly. "Maybe after years of the stuff you might be able to keep your balance better or something, but I don't think there's anything in *Denim Blues* that would demand us to know how to walk on a tightrope.

"Hey! What's going on?" Adam's familiar voice broke off the discussion. Caroline turned in Adam's direction, and in her smile Chrissy could see that she had forgotten her anger.

"When did you get here?" Caroline asked.

"Just now. How's the class going?"

"Don't ask," Chrissy replied. "I'm going to go change my clothes. I'll meet you two back here."

In the changing room, Chrissy tried to put the events of the past hour out of her head. Maybe that weirdo method worked for Caroline, but Chrissy decided it was definitely not her style. Somewhere there was the perfect approach for her to take, but it wasn't in one of Charles's classes. While Caroline and Adam were over at the Berkeley campus, she'd be able to study her lines with no distractions. *Besides*, Chrissy thought, *it's obvious that Adam and Caroline want to be alone.* "Who wants to be a third wheel?" she said to herself as she tied up her sneaker.

Outside, Adam and Caroline were deep into a discussion of acting methods. "I think I'll pass on the film archives," Chrissy told them.

"Are you sure?" Adam asked. "Can we persuade you to come to lunch with us?"

"Thanks, Adam," Chrissy said sincerely, "but I think I could use the afternoon to work on my lines." She turned to her cousin. "I really am sorry that I ruined your acting class, Cara."

"Well, I should have known better," Caroline admitted. "I was so excited about the class I didn't think that it might not be your kind of thing."

"Thanks for trying, anyway," Chrissy said, reassuring Caroline.

Caroline darted off to change into street clothes, while Chrissy headed for the door, double-checking her jacket pockets where she'd stuck her script earlier. She was glad to be spending the day by herself and bounded down the staircase into the afternoon sun.

The haze had burned off early, so the air was clear and everything looked green. She rode the cable car toward Nob Hill, where the Kirbys lived, but instead of going back to the apartment, Chrissy decided to go to a nearby park. It had turned into such a beautiful day, she decided to take advantage of the sunshine. With a great sigh, she plopped down on her special bench. She loved watching the children climb on the jungle gym and play in the sandboxes. Today she noticed a young couple throwing coins into one of the fountains. They looked enraptured and in love. Watching them made her think of the old days with Ben, back in Iowa. They were still close, but after experiencing a whole new way of life in California, Chrissy felt differently about Ben, and about living in Danbury. There was so much more to living than the farm.

Like making movies! she thought.

Sitting back on the bench, Chrissy pulled out the script from her pocket. She read through it again, imagining herself in the role of Shannon. It was an exciting scene, with some overtones of romance. *That's what I need right now,* Chrissy thought, *a little romance.*

The scene took place on the beach where she and Nick were picnicking. Nick's character, Eddie, was explaining that he'd have to go away for a while, but he'd be back at the end of the week. She read over the words, trying to memorize the script, but something seemed to be missing—the words just didn't ring true. She had imagined Shannon as being more dynamic and effervescent. *The one thing Shannon's not is a wimp,* Chrissy thought. She wouldn't say to Eddie

"Good luck, I'll be waiting for you"; she'd say "It doesn't matter how dangerous it is, I want to be with you, Eddie."

"Oh, that's much better," she said, quickly rummaging through her purse for a pencil. She scribbled down her new dialogue, then read it over. She was even more pleased with the change now. Then she'd throw her arms around his neck and passionately kiss him. Her mind was working faster than her hands could write. The creativity flowed and Chrissy finally stopped writing when she noticed the shadows of the swing stretching across the brick courtyard.

"There," she said, exaggerating the final period. She read over the scene again. *That's ten times better than the original,* she thought. *I wonder if Mr. Hayes would want to see this. He seemed like such a perfectionist when we saw him directing last Sunday. Maybe he'd like to see a new improved version of this scene.*

With that thought in mind, Chrissy ran to the print shop down the hill and copied the pages. Then she bought a large manila envelope at the stationery store and finally bought stamps and mailed the pages at the post office with a brief note in time for the five o'clock pickup. She hoped the audition address would be a good enough place to send it.

Chrissy walked home feeling good about her work. She couldn't wait to share her new script with Caroline. The whole character of Shannon was much better, she felt—more high-spirited, and fun. Chrissy caught her own reflection in the store windows and tried to imagine how Shannon would dress, walk, and talk. *I'm going to have to make a few changes,* she thought. *I wonder if Caroline would want me to rewrite her scene with Pete.*

At home there was a message from Caroline saying that she and Adam were going out for pizza and she'd most likely be home pretty late, so Chrissy ended up staying in their room most of the night rehearsing. Her mind was still full of thoughts of her scene when she pulled on Ben's old football jersey and climbed into bed. Instead of turning out the light, she opened her box of stationery and began a letter to her family:

"Dear Mom and Dad, Tom, Will, and Jimmy,
    "You'll never guess what! I'm a movie star!! Well, almost . . . "

Chrissy finished her letter ten minutes later, then signed it with a flourish and switched off her lamp. She was already half asleep when she heard Caroline come in.

"Chrissy, are you still awake?" she asked. "I had a fabulous time today with Adam." Chrissy rolled over and pretended to be asleep. She did want to hear about Adam, but right at that moment her own excitement had drained all her energy. Caroline didn't seem to notice, however, and Chrissy drifted off to sleep, listening to her cousin's excited chatter.

Chapter 10

Chrissy opened her weary eyes and glanced at the alarm clock on the nightstand. Seven A.M. *It's Sunday,* she thought to herself, *go back to sleep.* She rolled over and punched a soft spot into her pillow.

"Ah, ah, ah, ah, ah, oh, oh, oh," Caroline sang in a low-pitched voice from her perch on the window seat looking out at the Bay. Chrissy ignored the sound and pulled the sides of the pillows to cover her ears, but it didn't do any good.

"What are you doing?" Chrissy inquired, sitting upright in her bed.

Caroline turned her head in surprise to look at Chrissy. "Chrissy, I didn't wake you, did I? I'm sorry. I was trying to do my exercises quietly."

"More exercises?" Chrissy rolled her eyes.

"This is called vocalizing," Caroline explained. "I found this book at the Berkeley film library on acting techniques when I was with Adam yesterday, so I'm trying out some of their exercises."

"Caroline, it's seven o'clock on a Sunday morning. Go back to sleep." Chrissy rolled over and placed the pillow over her head again. The last thing she wanted to hear was an off-key cousin warbling in her ear.

"I'll try to be quieter," Caroline promised. She turned back to the window and began her exercises again. "You know, I can really feel my jaw muscle loosening up when I do this. Do you want to try? I'm sure you'd like the exercises in this book better than you liked Charles's class."

"Not now," Chrissy answered, puckering her lip at Caroline and still trying to retrieve her covers.

"Okay," Caroline answered. With a shrug she resumed her humming.

"Oh, what's the use?" Chrissy grumbled aloud to herself. "I'm awake now; I might as well get up." Chrissy flipped her legs to one side and reached for her robe at the foot of the bed.

"Wait, wait," Caroline said, jumping up from the window seat to push her cousin lightly back on the pillow. "Before you get up, why don't you do some early rising stretches? It's supposed to help you limber up for the rest of the day."

Chrissy sighed. She knew her cousin would be hurt if she didn't accept her help, especially since she'd asked for some acting tips last week. "Let me just get a glass of orange juice and then I'll stretch," she said.

"But you're supposed to stretch before you've eaten," Caroline said, holding Chrissy down gently by the shoulders. "Lay back down on the outside of the covers and breathe deeply."

"That's what I was doing before you made me get up," Chrissy complained. "Good night, Cara. . . ." Chrissy tried to pull the covers up, but now Caroline was determined.

"Just do what I tell you and I assure you you'll be sharper and more alive all day. It clears the mind and allows new energy to encircle the brain. It will help you memorize your script in half the time. The book guarantees it."

"What will it do for the circles under my eyes from lack of sleep?" Chrissy asked with a touch of sarcasm.

"Look, Chrissy, I'm just trying to help," Caroline said, putting her hands on her hips. "I thought you were really serious about wanting to be in the movie."

"I *am* serious," Chrissy replied.

"Well, then, why don't you want to do these exercises? This is what real actors do to relax and get in the mood for a part."

"I was relaxed before when I was sleeping!" Chrissy snuggled under the covers once more. "And that's exactly what I'm going to do right now."

"Suit yourself," Caroline said. She continued

with her vocalizing, but this time she made no effort to keep the noise down.

Under the covers, Chrissy couldn't sleep, and it wasn't only the noise that was bothering her. *Why does Cara always think she knows better than me?* she wondered. *I realize she's been taking these acting classes, but that doesn't make her an expert, especially if all she's been learning are these ridiculous exercises.* Peeking out from beneath her blanket, Chrissy saw her cousin tidying up her side of the room as she vocalized. *The acting techniques in that book are no better,* Chrissy thought. *I still don't see what any of these exercises has to do with acting. Is Cara going to perform her vocalizing for Mr. Hayes at the audition or something?* The thought made Chrissy giggle out loud.

"What's so funny?" Caroline asked.

"You."

Caroline glared at her. "You won't be laughing when all my acting exercises get me a part in the movie and you're still trying to sneak on to the set."

Chrissy took a deep breath and silently counted to ten, but when she'd reached ten she was still angry. "I don't think so, Cara. I think it's going to be the other way around," Chrissy retorted as she threw off her covers.

"I suppose you have another crazy plan."

"As a matter of fact, I do." Chrissy got up from the bed and began pacing around the room as she described her method. "I've rewritten the

script and I think it's fabulous. I sent a copy to Mr.
Hayes, and once he reads it, he's just got to feel
the same way. You see, I've made Shannon into a
really wild character—a real movie original. And
I'm going to show Mr. Hayes that Shannon is me,
so even before the audition he'll have decided
that I'm the one he wants."

"You're really serious about this, aren't you?"
Caroline said, sitting calmly on the edge of her
bed. "It'll never work in a million years." She
grinned. "Didn't you see how upset he was when
we fouled up his schedule last week? I can't
believe you honestly think you'll get ahead by
pulling some harebrained stunt."

"Harebrained," Chrissy echoed, starting to burn
again. "It can't be any more ridiculous than that
'ah-ah-ah, oh-oh-oh' stuff you've been doing."

"The best actors in the world do these warm-
ups before they perform."

"Yeah, in a circus, Cara. You look silly."

"Fine, but, like I said, we'll see how silly I look
when I'm doing the film and you're not."

"Thanks for the compliment, but don't be too
mad when I don't sign your autograph book,"
Chrissy fired back.

By now both girls were stomping and stamping
around the room, slamming doors, and gathering
up their clothes. Caroline took some pants out of
Chrissy's drawer.

"I guess if you don't like my acting, you won't
want to be borrowing any of my clothes either."

"And if my ideas are so wild," Chrissy retorted,

"you won't need to use any of my wild accessories." She snatched up a scarf, some earrings, and a necklace from Caroline's side of the dresser and returned it to her own.

"So, I guess this is it," Caroline declared. She grabbed her book on acting techniques. Then, giving Chrissy a superior glance, she stormed out of the room.

The battle lines had been drawn, and it didn't seem as if either girl had any plans of backing down. Chrissy hated fighting with Caroline. Since she'd arrived in San Francisco over a year ago, she and Caroline had gotten to know each other not only as cousins, but as best friends, too. What had she ever done before she'd discovered that she had a long-lost cousin almost exactly her own age? Sure she and Caroline had argued during the past year, but they'd always made up after just a short time. This time Chrissy knew their argument would last at least six days—until the audition on Saturday. She simply had to prove to her cousin that her crazy ideas could be successful. After all, it was one of her crazy ideas that had gotten them on to the film set last week, wasn't it?

I'm really going to have to come up with something spectacular now, Chrissy thought. *What can I do to make Mr. Hayes realize that I'm perfect for the part of Shannon?*

Thoughtfully, she walked over to the window seat and gazed out at the view. Although the morning was still foggy, she could see the Bay in the distance and even a few sailboats in the harbor. She thought about taking a walk down to the Wharf, or maybe back to her special park, but then suddenly Chrissy knew exactly how she would spend her Sunday.

Below her window, she heard the familiar sound of wheels skimming over the cracks in the sidewalk. Skateboarding—of course! Her face brightened. Hadn't Josh said that he was giving Nick lessons for some scenes in the movie? It would probably be a terrific advantage if Shannon could skateboard, too! *And Josh said he'd teach me to skateboard. Maybe he's got time today,* she thought hopefully as she showered in a hurry and then pulled her clothes on.

Still only eight-thirty, she noticed, glancing at the clock. *Too early to call on a Sunday. I'll wait until after breakfast.*

In the kitchen she found Caroline nibbling on toast and jelly, but neither girl said a word.

"You two are up early today," Aunt Edith said as she sauntered in wearing her bathrobe and carrying the Sunday newspaper. She poured herself some coffee and sat down. "I am so glad it's Sunday. Hey! Girls, how about if we all go to Sausalito for the day? Wouldn't that be nice?"

"I don't think so, Mom," Caroline said, glancing at Chrissy. "Maybe some other time."

"But it's supposed to be a lovely day today," Aunt Edith went on, "and we can scout new artists for the gallery at the Village Fair. Your father is already getting ready, and you know what it takes to drag him away from his Sunday papers."

"It sounds like fun, Aunt Edith, but I've already got something planned for today," Chrissy announced quietly. She glanced across the table and found her cousin glaring at her.

"I've changed my mind," Caroline declared. "I think I will go to Sausalito with you and Dad. It's been ages since I've been there."

As her aunt and Caroline talked about Sausalito, Chrissy concentrated on buttering her toast. She honestly would have liked to go to the quaint little town by the Bay, but not if Caroline was going to ignore her all day. Besides, she had an important mission to accomplish today.

"Excuse me," she began, putting down her half-eaten toast. "I have a call to make before I go out. Aunt Edith, have a good time in Sausalito," she added. As she left the kitchen, she caught her cousin's suspicious stare and had to smile. *Cara will never guess who I'm calling,* she thought with satisfaction, *and she'll never guess what I'm going to do today, either.*

In the hallway, Chrissy settled on the floor next to the telephone table and picked up the directory. "Brown—that's his last name," she mumbled to herself as she ran her finger down the long columns of "Browns." "Ugh!" She sighed. "John Brown, Joe Brown, Jerry Brown. I don't think he lives near Chinatown. . . ." Then she saw four J. Brown's listed. "Well, I might as well dive in." She started down the list and began dialing. The first two J. Brown's were not at all pleased to be interrupted on a Sunday morning. On the ninth ring of the third J. Brown, Chrissy thought she recognized Josh's voice. "Josh," she said hesitantly, "this is Chrissy—Chrissy Madden. You know, one of the girls on the set of *Denim Blues* last week. You showed us around," she prodded.

"Oh, yeah," he said, trying to clear his throat. "How could I forget?"

"I just called to thank you for being so nice last Sunday."

"That's all right," Josh replied. "Any time."

Chrissy took a deep breath. She hoped he remembered his offer. "I was wondering," she began. "Do you remember the casting call?"

"Yes. What about it?"

"Well, do you remember saying that you'd give me a skateboarding lesson?" she asked.

He laughed. "So you're calling to arrange a lesson." Josh paused. "Okay. When do you want it?"

Nervously Chrissy switched the phone to her other ear. "Is now too soon?" she asked.

"Right now?" he queried in surprise.

"Whenever you have the time." Chrissy tried not to sound too eager.

"Well . . . uh . . ." Josh stammered, then paused. "I'll tell you what," he continued after a moment. "Do you know the park at Union Square?"

"I sure do," Chrissy said excitedly.

"I'll meet you there in one hour. Wear some knee and elbow pads and bring your board."

"Great!" Chrissy exclaimed. "There's only one thing."

"What's that?"

"I haven't got a board."

Chrissy didn't hear anything on the other end. *He probably thinks either I'm a complete nut case or I've suddenly developed a crush on him*, she thought.

At last she heard a noise come over the wire. "If you don't have a board then you can use my old one. It's a bit wobbly, but you should be okay," he said quickly.

"That sounds fine," Chrissy replied. "See you in an hour."

A few minutes later Chrissy rounded the corner of Mason Street and saw a small group of "boarders" around their favorite hangout, a shop selling all kinds of equipment. On the floor was a bin of knee and elbow pads marked "Sale." Most of them were too small or too large, but after slipping on several different varieties, Chrissy found two neon orange knee pads and two green neon elbow pads. She plopped her money down quickly, then ran out to meet Josh.

When she was about three blocks away from Union Square, her heartbeat quickened and she felt extraordinarily excited. As she came into the south entrance of the park, she could see a group of students apparently giving an impromptu concert. Other than the singers, the square was fairly quiet, with only a handful of pigeons and Sunday strollers wandering about. Chrissy was glad of that—she wasn't too sure she wanted an audience just yet.

She sat on a bench and took the script out of her jacket pocket to read while she waited for Josh. As she quietly said the words of her new dialogue, a plan began to unfold. . . .

"Chrissy, Chrissy Madden," a voice called from behind.

"Hi," Chrissy answered, leaping up to meet Josh. As he walked toward her, she noticed the light playing through the streaks in his hair.

"I wasn't sure if I was dreaming or not. I was still pretty out of it when you called this morning," he said.

"I'm sorry. I know it was kind of early." She lowered her head and stuck her hands in her back pockets. "I really appreciate your helping me out with this, especially on such short notice."

"You trying to impress your boyfriend?" Josh inquired as he slipped on his safety gloves and pads, and noticed Chrissy do the same.

"No. I haven't really got a boyfriend," Chrissy answered.

"Oh. Well, then, why the sudden urge to learn how to skateboard?"

Chrissy was dying to tell someone her plan, but Josh worked too closely with Nick and Pete, and she didn't want anyone to find out until the audition.

"Learning to skateboard was one of my New Year's resolutions," she declared.

"Chrissy, it's almost November."

"Better late than never, I say," Chrissy replied with a shrug.

Josh gave her an odd look, and Chrissy had to suppress the smile brimming within her at the thought of Josh's reaction when she put her plan into action.

"Well, let's get started," he said. "This is the board," he said, bringing out a large slab curved up at one end. "It's thirty-one inches of laminated maple on wheels. These can be very dangerous, so that's why I insist on the pads. When you start twist-jumps and handstands, a helmet is essential." He tapped Chrissy on the shoulder and smiled. "Have you ever ridden on one of these things before?"

"Never," Chrissy said, shrugging.

"Then we'll start with the basics. It's similar to surfing, but with wheels." He set the board down and instructed Chrissy to stand on it.

"Whoa!" she screamed, holding onto his arm. "This thing wobbles."

"It's supposed to. When you get better on it you can use those wobbles to your advantage. It helps with turns, velocity, and tricks."

"I can't even stand on it. You won't let go, will you?" Chrissy asked him in a shaky voice.

"Not until you get the feel of it. Set your left foot in the back a little at an angle. Then place your right leg up in front. That's it."

Chrissy shifted herself into the position Josh had described and tried to balance her weight.

For the next hour, Josh had Chrissy do various stances on the board, just to get used to it. "Left foot on." "Right foot off." "Weight in the front." "Rock the board gently." Chrissy began to feel comfortable on the board as long as she could still clutch onto Josh's arm for support.

"Okay, Chrissy, I think you've basically mastered the skate board."

"That wasn't so hard," Chrissy remarked.

"I meant in a stationary position."

"Oh." Chrissy laughed, a little embarrassed. "I'm not sure I'm ready for it to roll."

"Before you know it, you'll be another Tony Hawk, doing fancy tricks like his Varials and the Frigidaire."

"If you say so," Chrissy said, getting excited about it.

"Okay, let's roll. Set your right foot in the center of the board a little to the front." Chrissy did so, keeping her balance with the left foot on the ground. "Now, using your left foot, push off gently, like you would on a scooter."

Josh let go of her right arm and she softly pushed off with her left foot, gliding slowly on the pavement.

"Good job, Chrissy!" Josh cheered. "Now try it again, but instead, put your left foot back on the board. Don't forget to use your arms for balance."

Chrissy shoved off much harder than the first time, and before she knew it, the board was sliding forward, while she hit tail first on the pavement. "Ouch!" Chrissy groaned in pain. "What happened?"

"You took your first fall—a real hard one, too. Are you okay?" His blue eyes sparkled, and even through her embarrassment, Chrissy was touched by his compassion. "Anything broken?"

"Just my ego hurts," Chrissy said, forcing a smile. "To tell the truth, I think I'm wearing my pads in the wrong place. Oooh, that smarts," she continued, as Josh helped her get back on her feet. "Maybe I should rest awhile." Chrissy limped toward the nearest park bench and tried to find a comfortable position in which to sit.

"Oh, no, you don't, kiddo," Josh said, taking Chrissy's arm. "It's just like horseback riding—you have to get right back on and try again. Come on, I'll help you." Gingerly, he put his arm around Chrissy's waist and led her back to the grassy spot where her board was lying upside down.

"Here you go," he said, setting the board back on its wheels. "Now this time take it easy."

Chrissy rubbed her numb backside and stepped on the board. This time she was careful not to let her enthusiasm—and the board—carry her away. With a short, smooth rhythm, she pushed and glided along the cement. When she felt the board give, she tried shifting her weight, rocking it into an easy turn. "This is fun!" she cried, sailing along to the beat of the singing chorus. "The music really helps."

As Chrissy guided the board down the sidewalk, she gained confidence and speed. *I'm really doing it!* she thought in amazement. She stared down at her feet, feeling the whirring wheels beneath them. When she finally looked up, she realized she was headed directly toward the group of singers at the south enterance

They had reached the chorus of "Blowin' in the Wind" and the leader, a tall, serious-looking boy, was beckoning the few spectators to sing along, when Chrissy shouted, "Watch out!"

The spectators fled to either side of the sidewalk, but the singers just kept singing as Chrissy zoomed straight for them.

"Please move!" she yelled. "I can't stop this thing!"

With a nod from the song leader, the singers were quiet. They stared at Chrissy for a moment. Then, as if on cue, they divided, leaving a clear path for her. She breathed a sigh of relief—but the next thing she knew, she was flying off the skateboard and smack into the very angry and embarrassed song leader.

"Are you okay?" Josh asked, racing to Chrissy's rescue. "I shouldn't laugh, but that was one of the funniest things I have ever seen. Why didn't you stop?"

"Because I don't know how," Chrissy said dryly as she scrambled to her feet. She rubbed her bruised shoulder. "You know, what I really feel like doing right now is soaking in a hot tub, but if I'm ever going to skateboard again, you'd better teach me how to stop or I'll be in big trouble."

Josh nodded in agreement and continued the lesson. Although Chrissy got a few more bumps and bruises, by the end of the day she felt ready to continue with the next part of her plan. The only question was when.

Chapter 11

During the week Chrissy split her time between rehearsing her script and practicing on the old skateboard Josh had lent her. She also crammed in time for her homework—especially trig. She didn't want to disappoint Mr. Turner again.

Even though she was busy, Chrissy still missed Caroline's company. They rarely crossed paths these days, even in the apartment—but when they did, they said as little as possible to each other. Chrissy was sure that Aunt Edith and Uncle Richard must have noticed the uncomfortable atmosphere, but much to her relief, they went on acting like normal.

Chrissy knew that the kids at school had sensed the tension between herself and Caroline, but they were all so involved in their own activities that she didn't see much of them during the week anyway. Tracy and Maria were helping Justine come up with new ideas for scholarship fund raisers, while Justine had also lassoed Randy into helping her memorize her lines. The auditions were the talk of the school, and for Chrissy Saturday couldn't arrive soon enough.

Today's the day, Chrissy thought as she started setting out her clothes for the afternoon's audition. It had taken a week of careful planning to come up with the right look to land her the part of Shannon. She could almost hear Caroline laughing at her as she put out the shirt she'd bought to wear. It was bright yellow with patches of blue, green, and red, and a sequined sunset was stitched on the back. It was wild, but so was Shannon—especially in the scene Chrissy had rewritten for her audition. Unfortunately, she hadn't had enough money for a new pair of pants to go with the shirt, so her red stretch stirrup pants would have to do for the bottom half. She knew Caroline's bright blue ones would have been better, but she didn't dare ask. Besides, she knew her cousin had left the house earlier.

Chrissy surveyed her outfit with a smile. *And now to get my hair done up Shannon-style to match my wild, Shannon-style outfit,* she thought, grabbing her jacket and yelling a quick good-bye to her uncle.

Normally Chrissy went to the same hair salon

as Caroline for a simple trim of her long blond hair, but this time she wanted something a bit different. Earlier in the week she had read an ad in a local magazine for Stephanie's Scissors, and she'd decided that it was Shannon's kind of place. The ad had said: "Long or short, spikes or stripes—we'll cut it, color it, or curl it at Stephanie's Scissors."

Now as Chrissy raced up the hill to catch the cable car, she still couldn't decide how she should have her hair done. *Well, I guess I'll let the experts at Stephanie's Scissors decide. They'll know best, anyway,* she told herself as the cable car clanged to a stop.

The ride was short, but as always, Chrissy felt rejuvenated when she stepped off and looked down at the brightly colored boutiques that dotted Fillmore Street. After only a few blocks of walking, she found Stephanie's Scissors in the basement of a trendy shop. She descended the short flight of stairs and peered in the window at the arrangement of wigs, makeup, and outrageous hair accessories. "Shannon would love this place," she whispered to herself as she stepped into the doorway.

Inside, the walls were painted with brightly colored murals, reminding Chrissy of a kindergarten classroom. Vinelike plants hung from the sky-blue ceiling, and green-vinyl-covered chairs were parked in front of a long red counter. The hairdressers looked like rock stars, with their heavy makeup, flashy clothes, and, of course, their hip hairstyles. They even worked to the beat of the music blaring through the room.

Chrissy smiled to the receptionist and tried not to stare, as the girl continued talking on the telephone. The receptionist had very short razor-chopped purplish hair and wore five earrings in each ear, along with a tiny diamond stud in her nose.

"I was wondering if there was someone here who could help me with my hair," Chrissy said when the receptionist had hung up the phone.

"I can see why," she said. "You really need a lift. I think Piker's free for a while. I'll see if she can take you."

"That would be great," Chrissy replied, the smile still pasted on her face. *Piker?* she thought. *Maybe this place is a little too wild even for Shannon!* Then a voice in her head scolded her. *Don't chicken out, Chrissy. Shannon wouldn't chicken out, would she? No, you're right,* she told the voice. *Shannon's got guts. I wonder how much this is going to cost, anyway.*

As the receptionist walked toward the back of the salon, the heels on her purple fringed boots clicked against the tiled floor and her silver jewelry jangled. *Wow! That's some outfit,* Chrissy thought, taking in the girl's red leather miniskirt and vest. The red outfit seemed as if it would clash with her purple hair and boots, but on the receptionist it somehow looked right.

"Piker said you should come on back," she told Chrissy after a minute.

Chrissy nodded and followed the receptionist to the back of the salon, where Piker was waiting.

Piker turned out to be a very thin woman dressed completely in black—from the beret on her dyed black hair to her black jumpsuit and shoes. She certainly made a stark contrast to the brightly decorated salon.

"What can I do for you today?" Piker asked in a high-pitched voice.

"Well," Chrissy started out slowly, "I think my hair needs a lift."

Piker nodded and began to circle Chrissy, studying her carefully. She ran her fingers through the back of Chrissy's hair, bringing it out to its full length. When she'd made a full circle, she stopped to face Chrissy.

"Is this change for anything special?" she asked.

"As a matter of fact, it is," Chrissy replied. Explaining that her audition for *Denim Blues* was that afternoon, she ended by saying, "So, you see, I want my hair to look wild for the audition— like Shannon's. But I don't want much cut off, and I don't want to have to wear spikes or whatever all the time."

Piker smiled, lighting up her pale face. "Don't worry, I know just the thing. Are you really auditioning for a movie?" she asked, as she wrapped a plastic cape around Chrissy's shoulders and tied it at the back.

"Yup," Chrissy said, relaxing into the vinyl

chair, "and it stars Nick Matthews and Pete Becker."

"No kidding," Piker replied in awe. "Well, honey, I'm going to make you into the best Shannon around. Then you'll be sure to get the part."

For the next hour and a half, Chrissy put her trust in Piker, who teased, sprayed, pulled, and shaped her hair in every possible direction. Chrissy was dying to know what she looked like, but Piker wouldn't let her see until the makeover was complete.

As Piker was working, some of the other employees came over to watch and talk, and Piker told them all about Chrissy's audition. Cleo, the makeup artist at Stephanie's Scissors, was so thrilled that she offered to do Chrissy's face free of charge. After a few touches of glitz and glitter, Chrissy was allowed at last to peek in the mirror.

Her first reaction was one of total shock. "Holy mazoley!" she said softly. Her blond hair was puffed out all around her head for what must have been six inches. Chrissy decided she looked like a giant Q-tip, and she wanted to cry. Slowly she reached up her hand to touch it. *It doesn't even feel like hair,* she thought. *What am I going to do? I'm not even going to be able to fit through the door.* She looked back at her reflection and noticed tiny flecks on her eyes gleaming beneath the lights. She looked closer and realized that Cleo had applied a glittery gold shadow to her eyelids. It looked awful. Chrissy's face felt warm and she was having a difficult time swallowing. *Is that really me?* she thought.

"Well, Shannon, what do you think?" Piker asked.

Chrissy shut her eyes for a moment and thought about Shannon, the character she'd created in her scene. *That person in the mirror isn't supposed to be me,* she thought. *It's supposed to be Shannon.* Chrissy opened her eyes. Yes, that face staring back at her certainly did look like Shannon. Gradually, Chrissy's heartbeat slowed down to normal, and her expression transpired from panic to pleasure.

"Shannon thinks it's absolutely awesome," Chrissy said, making her voice sound husky, the way she imagined Shannon's voice to be. "It's perfect. I just have to think of myself as Shannon."

"We'll have our fingers crossed for you this afternoon," Cleo told her.

"Thanks," Chrissy said, stepping out of the chair and getting ready to leave. "What do I owe you?"

"Just an autographed picture of yourself when you become a star," Piker replied.

Grinning, Chrissy waved, then ran out and up the steps to the street.

As Chrissy opened the door to the apartment half an hour later, she heard her Uncle Richard typing away in the living room. She peeked in and saw him sitting at his desk in the corner wearing a pair of earphones, his fingers flying across the keys of the typewriter.

Uh-oh, he's working—probably typing his review of last night's symphony. I don't know how he can tell one symphony from another, considering all the concerts he goes to, she mused. *He must have one terrific ear in order to write his review column for the newspaper. Well, I'd better not bother him,* she thought.

But it was too late.

"Chrissy? Is that you?" he asked in surprise.

"Yup, it's me, Uncle Richard," she replied, self-consciously touching a hand to her billowing hair as she walked in the room. "What do you think?"

Uncle Richard gazed at her for a moment, then chuckled. "It sure looks like you've got your head in the clouds, Chrissy. I'll say that much."

If anyone else had made fun of her like that, Chrissy would have taken offense, but Uncle Richard was so good-natured, she couldn't help but smile.

"There was a call for you while you were out," he went on. "I think I got the message right. It's on the telephone table."

Chrissy went out to the hallway and scanned the note on the table. *Am I dreaming?* she wondered, reading the note again. Her uncle's handwriting was awful, but there was no mistaking the meaning of the message:

I have your work and everything looks great. We have a solid foundation for big plans ahead. Let's get together and talk.

Justin

Holding the note in a trembling hand, Chrissy brought it in to her uncle. "Is this the message?" she asked.

He nodded. "Sure is. It sounded important."

"Oh, thank you, Uncle Richard. That's the best message I've ever gotten!" Chrissy exclaimed, giving him a hug. "This is precisely what I needed."

"That's good," Uncle Richard replied with a puzzled expression. He shrugged and went back to his typewriter as Chrissy scurried to her bedroom to prepare the final details for her audition. Now that she knew for sure that Justin liked her script, she wanted to talk to him as soon as possible.

Darn! He's in the middle of auditions, she thought. *Well, this is more important than the auditions right now. Once we discuss the changes I've made in Shannon's character, he'll see that I'm the perfect girl for the part. Then he'd only have to audition girls to play Julie, but if I put in a good word for Cara, then we can both be in the movie.* The scenario fresh in her mind, Chrissy took out the packet Adam had given her at the casting call and looked up the phone number of the place where the tryouts were being held. She picked up the phone and dialed.

"Hello. May I help you?" a woman answered on the other end.

"Most definitely," Chrissy replied in her most mature voice. "I need to speak with Mr. Hayes."

"He's in auditions right now and can't be disturbed," the secretary replied.

"Yes, I know all about that, but I'm returning his call. I'm one of the scriptwriters of *Denim Blues* and I need to get in touch with him as soon as possible to discuss some changes."

"Does he have your name and number?" the woman asked.

"I believe so, but I'll give it to you just in case." Chrissy gave the woman her name and phone number and told her that it was important for Justin to get the message right away.

"They'll be taking their lunch break at one," she informed Chrissy. "His reservations are at the Portofino Caffè. You might be able to catch him there."

"That's splendid. Thank you very much," Chrissy said, then hung up the phone.

She jumped to her feet and danced a little jig around the room.

"There's no business like show business," she warbled, prancing around the room as she changed into her audition clothes. "Not bad, Shannon. Not bad at all," she whispered to her reflection. She shoved her safety pads into her book bag, along with her script and her precious message, then tucked Josh's skateboard under her arm and heaved a deep sigh.

That's everything, Chrissy thought. *I'm as ready as I'll ever be.* Her stomach fluttered and for a moment her muscles felt weak. Then a surge of excited energy flowed through her.

Good-bye, Chrissy Madden, plain old ordinary high school student. Hello, Chrissy Madden, movie star!

Chapter 12

Five minutes past one. Chrissy checked her watch and leaned up against a Victorian-style lamppost at the end of the Hyde Street trolley terminal. *Good. I'll give Justin a chance to start eating. Then I'll surprise him at Portofino's. I wouldn't want to interrupt him while he's got an empty stomach*, she thought. Even though she'd gotten that message from Justin, she was still nervous about discussing her script with him. After all, he was a Hollywood director—compared to him, what did she know about movies? *He must think I know something*, she reassured herself, *or he wouldn't have called.*

At ten past one, Chrissy picked up her belongings from the sidewalk and hurried the short distance to Ghirardelli Square, where she knew the Portofino Caffè was located. As she climbed the steps to the Square, Chrissy noticed a group of people stop to stare at her. At first she couldn't understand why, but then she realized that with her fluffy blond mane, heavy makeup, and loud shirt, she certainly might look a bit out of the ordinary. *Tourists*, she thought. *I wonder if they know I'm on my way to a meeting with a V.I.P. And if everything goes well, I'll be a V.I.P. myself soon!*

Smiling at the thought, Chrissy dashed up the rest of the steps and entered one of the old brick buildings that used to belong to the Ghirardelli chocolate company. Inside she slowed down and switched her skateboard and book bag to opposite arms. With a quick glance at her reflection in a shop window, she made her way to the Portofino Caffè on the second-floor terrace. To her relief, she saw Justin right away, sitting at a table with another man and a woman, and nibbling on a cracked crab.

"Justin," Chrissy called. She wasn't really sure if she should call him "Justin" or "Mr. Hayes," but since he'd left his name on the message as "Justin," Chrissy figured it was okay. She waved to the director, trying to catch his attention.

But before she could take another step forward, the maître d' grabbed her under her arm and led her off the patio.

"Hey! What do you think you're doing?" Chrissy asked, pulling her arm away.

"We don't want our customers being bothered.

If you'd like a table, please wait to be seated."

"Yes, I would like to be seated," Chrissy declared haughtily. "I'd like to be seated at Mr. Hayes's table, please. I'm sure if you tell him that Chrissy Madden is here, it will be all right. You tell him that I've received his message and I'm ready to discuss the script." The maître d' grunted and shrugged his shoulders, but walked over to the Hayes table. Chrissy stood on tiptoes to peer over the other tables and strained to see Mr. Hayes's reaction. Although she couldn't see his face clearly, she felt certain that he was anxious to have her join him.

But the maître d' returned wearing an expression that said "I told you so." "Mr. Hayes says he left no message and doesn't want to be disturbed," he informed her.

Chrissy was stunned. "Are you sure that's what he said?"

The maître d' nodded. "Yes, miss, I am quite sure. If you like, I can seat you at another table," he said with a smirk.

"No, thank you," Chrissy replied curtly. Pointing her nose in the air, she walked away.

I don't get it. I bet that snooty guy didn't tell Justin what I said. Chrissy wandered back toward the stairway leading to the first floor and sat on the top step. This time she ignored the funny looks she got from the passersby as she mulled over her predicament.

What am I going to do now? Chrissy wondered. *I don't want to wait until my audition to have a chance to talk to Justin. That's a few hours away, and by then he might have started thinking that I'm not interested.* She glanced up at the entrance to Portofino's, where she could see the maître d' still standing in the doorway. *Darn it! I'm sure if Justin knew I was here, he'd want to talk to me. He'd probably even treat me to lunch.*

At that thought, Chrissy realized her stomach was grumbling. She'd eaten her usual cereal and toast for breakfast, but that seemed like ages ago. And now the delicious scents emanating from Portofino's were making her mouth water. *They might have a grouchy maître d', but it sure smells like they've got a terrific chef,* she thought wistfully.

Opening her book bag, Chrissy plunged her hand down to the bottom until she grasped a folded-up piece of paper. She pulled out the telephone message and read it again. *It's right here—"Let's get together and talk." That does it! I'm going into Portofino's to try again. I've just got to see him, or I might miss out on the chance of a lifetime.*

With a renewed sense of determination, Chrissy stuffed her skateboard into her book bag with the safety pads and neatly folded message. Although her book bag was fairly large, it still left about one-third of the board exposed. *Well, at least it's not quite as obvious as before,* she thought, lifting the heavy bag to her shoulder. Then, following closely behind a trio of young well-dressed shoppers, she managed to get past

the entrance to Portofino's without being seen
and hide just around the corner, where she had a
perfect view of the restaurant.

She had to wait only a few minutes before the
maître d' was called away from his post at the
door. Without a moment's hesitation, she made a
beeline into Portofino's—past tables of elegant-
looking people dining on elegant-looking
dishes—hurrying to reach Justin's table before
the maître d' spotted her.

As Chrissy approached the table, she realized
that Justin's companions were two of the producers she had seen on the film set a couple of
weeks ago. *Oh, no,* she thought, but instead of
abandoning her mission, Chrissy resolved to daz-
zle all three movie moguls so that they'd never
forget her. She headed straight for the extra seat
at their table and sat down as if they should have
been expecting her.

Justin and the producers abruptly stopped talking and stared at her.

"Good afternoon, Mr. Hayes," Chrissy said, trying to sound confident. She set her book bag
down by her feet. "Sorry to interrupt your lunch,
but I wanted to talk to you about the script
changes I made." She put out her hand to shake
his, but when he didn't return the gesture, she
rushed ahead with her prepared speech. "I'm
Chrissy Madden. You left that message for me,
remember? I hope you don't mind if I—"

"Excuse me, miss, but we *do* mind," one of the
producers objected. He took a puff of his cigar.

"Perhaps you could make an appointment to speak with Mr. Hayes later so we can finish our lunch."

"I don't mind if you keep eating," Chrissy assured him. "It's just that I wanted to talk to Mr. Hayes as soon as possible." She glanced across the table at Justin, who was still staring at her and chewing his cracked crab very slowly. "I'm glad you like the changes I've made in the script. . . ."

At this, the other producer choked on her wine. "Changes? What changes, Justin?"

Justin threw up his hands in a puzzled gesture, but before he could defend himself, the producers began bombarding him with reasons why he couldn't make changes in the script.

"More revisions means more money."

"And time. Justin, we've already spent six months perfecting the script."

"We've got Matthews and Becker starring. Who cares about the script? Let's get the darned show on the road, Justin."

"Agnes is right. Besides, all the writers in Hollywood have been warned off this project now. Where would we find another writer even if we wanted to?"

"Right here," Chrissy declared loudly. At last she'd got their attention. "I've rewritten one scene already. That's what I came here to discuss with Justin."

All eyes turned to Justin. He seemed at a loss for a moment, like a little boy being scolded for something he didn't do. Then suddenly he straightened his slumped shoulders and narrowed his eyes at Chrissy. "I know who you are," he said. "You're one of the girls we found trespassing on the set a few weeks ago. Aren't you?"

Chrissy nodded. She couldn't understand why she detected a harsh tone to his voice. *He did say he wanted to get together and talk,* she thought. *I guess he wanted to talk in private, though, so we could work out the changes first. Then he could have presented the revisions already complete and avoided this hassle.* She noticed Justin's face getting redder and his chest heaving as he glared at her. *He must be putting on this act for the benefit of the producers,* she decided. *He's not bad. Maybe he should be an actor instead of a director.*

"Young lady," Justin growled, "I don't know what you're talking about, but I suggest you leave this table right now."

He really seems serious, Chrissy thought, a feeling of panic building up inside her. Fidgeting under the menacing stares of three pairs of eyes, she accidentally knocked over her book bag with her foot. It landed with a thud and a familiar whirring sound. Chrissy's eyes lit up. Of course!

Justin cleared his throat. "Young lady, I'm afraid if you don't leave now, we'll have you escorted out. And I mean it!" he barked.

"Yes, sir, I understand," Chrissy replied calmly, although inside she was trembling. As she spoke, she reached under the tablecloth and pretended to scratch her leg. "I also understand that Nick Matthews is learning to skateboard for his part in *Denim Blues*. It's only logical that maybe his girl friend, Shannon, should be able to skateboard, too. That way, they'd have a common bond and they could go skateboarding all over town together." *Get to the point, Chrissy,* she told herself, as she noticed her audience getting even more impatient. "And as a matter of fact, I happen to be an expert skateboarder," she declared, whipping out the skateboard from beneath the table-cloth.

As she set the board on the floor and balanced herself on top of it, the two producers stared openmouthed, and Justin's chest heaved more rapidly.

Suddenly he let out a holler that would have registered on the Richter scale. "Get out of here! Get out of my sight!" he screamed.

The force of Justin's voice caused Chrissy to lose her concentration and the board slid out from under her. She fell backward, smack into a waiter carrying a trayful of food. Water pitchers, fruit cups, and silverware scattered as the waiter lost his balance, staggered backward, then forward, and finally landed in a dessert cart. Meanwhile, the skateboard had crashed into a potted geranium.

Chrissy surveyed the scene and felt like crying. *I've really messed up this time,* she thought as the maître d' escorted her to the door.

Chapter 13

Chrissy's knees were still shaking when she reached the bottom step of Ghirardelli Square. A waiter followed behind her, delivering the skateboard. He didn't say a word, just made a humphing sound, then headed back toward the restaurant. Chrissy clutched the board in one hand and the book bag in the other and ran to the nearest bus stop. She wanted to get far, far away from Portofino's. Without a second thought, she hopped on the first bus without even checking to find out where it was headed.

Maybe the bus will take me back to Iowa, she thought wistfully. *Wouldn't that be terrific? Then I could forget about this whole fiasco and go back to being good old Chrissy Madden, captain of the cheerleaders, B student, and Ben Hatcher's girl.*

*Life was so much easier then. No Hollywood
hotshots ever came to Danbury to make movies,
that's for sure. If it weren't for that darned
tornado, I'd be home right now. Why couldn't
Mom and Dad have let me come home anyway? I
think I'd even rather be staying at Uncle Ned's
with the boys than staying here.*

As the bus rumbled up and down the hills of
San Francisco, Chrissy gazed out the window, but
her mind was on things other than the scenery.
*Not only have I completely messed up my one big
chance to be a movie star and act in a movie with
Nick Matthews, but I've completely messed up my
relationship with Cara. I'll bet she had a wonderful audition. She'd be absolutely perfect for the
part of Julie, and with all her hard work and
dedication, she really deserves that part. I only
wish I'd followed her example—then maybe I'd
still have a chance.*

Just then the bus stopped at a traffic light, and
Chrissy realized that she was very close to
Golden Gate Park. If she got off at the next stop,
she'd have only a short walk to the Japanese tea
garden. *That's as good a place as any to drown
my sorrows,* she decided, pulling the buzzer for
the bus to stop.

This time Chrissy paid the dollar admission and
walked through the main entrance to the beauti-
fully landscaped garden. It seemed much different without all the film equipment, trailers, tents,
and, most of all, the people they'd gotten to know
that day on the set of *Denim Blues*. Would she

ever see Nick again? she wondered, as she rounded the pagoda and took a seat on a nearby bench. Probably she'd just call Josh to return his skateboard and ask him to tell Nick good-bye. She'd always remember Nick in a special way, but would he just think of her as one of his groupies?

"Excuse me, miss." A quiet voice interrupted Chrissy's mood. "Are you saving this bench for anyone else?" Chrissy looked up and couldn't believe her eyes.

"Cara," she said, staring up at her cousin.

"Chrissy?" Caroline answered, peering back. "Is that you?" Caroline sat on the bench next to Chrissy. "What have you done to your hair?" she asked.

"Oh, this," Chrissy said, self-consciously patting her fluffy hairdo. "I did it for the audition."

"Oh," Caroline replied quietly, looking away. For a moment neither girl said anything as they gazed across the garden.

"So, how was your audition?" Chrissy asked finally, turning toward her cousin. She was prepared to get both barrels and wanted to look Caroline straight in the eye.

"Oh, fine," Caroline answered nonchalantly.

"Did you read from the script?"

"Oh, yes." Caroline nodded.

"I'll bet it was a big help having Adam and Pete there to give you moral support," Chrissy remarked.

"Well, Pete was . . . was speechless," Caroline said. "And Adam . . ." She paused, and Chrissy noticed a flicker of a smile cross her cousin's face. "He's been wonderful all week, and especially today."

Chrissy tried to act happy. It was nice of Caroline not to be bragging about her audition, she thought.

"How about you?" Caroline asked. "How was your audition? Was it as unique as you planned?"

"Uniquer," Chrissy responded, turning to face the pagoda.

"No kidding. What did Mr. Hayes say?"

"Well, I think I really surprised him."

"Wow!" Caroline exclaimed. "You must have really made an impression."

"Unforgettable," Chrissy admitted. She sighed and focused her eyes on the pagoda. She could imagine herself having a secret meeting there with Nick, then walking hand in hand down to the little Japanese bridge. They'd kiss. Then Justin would shout "Cut! That's a take." But that would never happen now. Perhaps Cara would let her come down to the set to watch the filming."When do you start filming?" she asked.

Caroline gave her a puzzled look. "What do you mean?"

"Huh?" Chrissy was dumbfounded. "I thought you got the part?"

"Hardly," Caroline confessed, still facing Chrissy. "You were right—my method was a complete disaster. I looked like an old maid in this dumb suit," she said, glancing down at her conservative skirt and blazer, "and Justin didn't even acknowledge my existence. He sat reading a newspaper, while one of his assistants read off *one* line."

"One line?" Chrissy echoed. "But I thought you were supposed to read with Pete. You just said he was speechless."

"That's because he wasn't even there. I don't think Mr. Hayes ever intended for Pete and Nick to read with us."

"Somehow, I'm not surprised anymore," Chrissy grumbled.

"I overheard someone say that Pete and Nick were supposed to be doing publicity shots here in the tea garden sometime this afternoon. That's why I came here, but I don't see them," she said, glancing around. "I just wanted to see Pete one more time. You know, Chrissy, you were absolutely right. All those dumb exercises I learned in Charles's class and in that book on acting—none of that stuff helps at all when it comes to getting a part."

"Neither does the wild and wacky method," Chrissy admitted.

"You mean your audition didn't go well either?"

"Not only didn't it go—I never even had one."

"Oh, Chrissy." Caroline gasped sympathetically. "Why not? What happened?"

Chrissy took a deep breath. "The whole thing was a complete disaster. You know I rewrote that scene for the audition."

Caroline nodded. "I heard you rehearsing last week."

"Well, I sent the scene to Justin, and today I got a message from him saying that everything looked great and he wanted to get together to talk." Chrissy dug into her book bag and pulled out the message. "Here, look," she said, handing it to Caroline.

As Caroline read the message, her expression changed from curiosity to dismay. "Chrissy, this message is from Just*ine*, not Justin."

A cold wave of panic washed over Chrissy. *Cara must be mistaken*, she thought. *I'm sure that message was from Justin.* But deep inside, she knew her cousin could be right.

"Chrissy, do you see that little loop on the end of where it says Justin? That's how my dad makes his *e*'s," Caroline went on. "And when I saw Justine at the audition, she said she tried to call you so you two could talk about plans for more fund raisers for the scholarship fund. She says she likes your ideas a lot and has some of her own."

Chrissy didn't know what to say. Suddenly she couldn't sit still. Slowly she got up from the bench and wandered aimlessly along the path. *How could I have been so stupid?* she wondered. *I can't blame Justin—Mr. Hayes—for getting so angry with me. Not only did I ruin his lunch, I very nearly ruined his career.*

Behind her, Chrissy could hear the click-clack of Caroline's heels on the pavement. She stopped on the Japanese bridge to wait for her cousin.

There was no point in taking out her anger at her own stupidity on Caroline.

"Oh, Cara, I've really made a fool of myself this time," Chrissy groaned. She leaned on the railing of the bridge and put her head in her hands. "If you could have seen Justin's face—it was bright pink, like the inside of a watermelon. And those producers—I think they must have thought I'd stepped out of one of those slapstick comedies." At the memory of her episode at Portofino's, Chrissy couldn't help but giggle.

Caroline put her arm around Chrissy to soothe her. "Don't worry, Chrissy. I'm sure it couldn't have been that bad."

"But it was," Chrissy said in between giggles.

"But there's no need to cry about it. Honestly, Chrissy . . ."

Chrissy looked up at her cousin's worried face, but it only made her laugh harder.

"Chrissy Madden, you're not funny! I thought you were really upset!" Caroline shouted.

"I was, Cara, but holy cow, this is just too funny." With that, she proceeded to tell her cousin exactly what had happened—interspersed with lots of laughter. By the time she was through with her story, Caroline was laughing, too. As they shrieked and giggled, a crowd gathered around the bridge watching them. Chrissy was laughing so hard her eyes were tearing.

She stepped backward, imitating the waiter at Portofino's, but instead of falling in a dessert cart, her foot landed on the pebbles next to one end of the bridge. As she slid down into the stream, Caroline reached down her hand to help.

"Hold on, Chrissy!" she called. And hold on Chrissy did, pulling Caroline into the stream with her.

Suddenly, two figures dove into the water and swam to save Chrissy and Caroline.

"Hey! What's going on?" Chrissy cried, as a large arm encircled her body.

"Don't worry, I've got you!" someone shouted into Chrissy's ear.

"Just relax," said the other man, placing his hand under Caroline's chin and forcing her into a floating position.

"I know how to swim," Caroline said, resisting him. But the men's arms were too strong, and the girls eventually allowed themselves to be rescued.

When they hit the shore, Chrissy's rescuer flung her over his shoulder like a sack of potatoes. Caroline did not escape similar treatment.

"I know how to swim. You really didn't have to go through all that," Caroline repeated, as he started to lower her onto the grass face first.

"I wasn't drowning," Chrissy added, kicking her legs while the strong arms set her down on the ground. Chrissy was face to face now with her savior. "Nick!" she squealed before starting to choke. Quickly Nick cocked her head back, pinched her nose, and began giving her artificial respiration. Caught up in the moment, Chrissy threw her arms around Nick's neck and turned his first-aid attempt into a kiss, which Nick returned.

Meanwhile, Pete pushed down firmly on Caroline's back to make sure there was no water trapped in her lungs. When he was sure she was all right, he flipped Caroline over and revealed his identity to her. He hugged her and the crowd cheered its approval.

"This is great," a man called from the front of the group. "Keep those cameras rolling. I think we've got our publicity shot."

"Are you all right, sunshine?" Nick asked after a prolonged kiss.

"Yes, Nick, but I'm such a mess!" Chrissy said, embarrassed, trying to explain her appearance.

"How did you get in the water?" Pete asked Caroline. They looked knowingly at each other.

"Chrissy," they answered together, laughing.

The crowd soon dispersed, leaving the couples and the camera crew standing by the shore.

"Let's get a shot of this," the cameraman called to the reporter. "I can see the headline now: 'Teen Stars Save Lives of Local Fans.'"

"Oh, no! Not pictures!" Caroline gasped, trying to wipe off the mascara and eyeliner that had run down her cheeks.

"I thought you wanted to be a movie star," Pete joked, helping Caroline dab her eyes with the handkerchief.

"Not looking like this," she answered, attempting unsuccessfully to straighten her soggy clothing.

Meanwhile, Chrissy wrung out her shirt. "I guess I thought my debut would be a bit more glamorous."

"Okay, everybody," the photographer called. "Look here and say 'Cheese!'"

Chapter 14

"Extra! Extra! Read all about it!" Aunt Edith announced cheerily, poking her head into the girl's room early Sunday morning. "Hey, you sleepyheads, you made the front page!"

"What?" Chrissy grumbled, trying to wake up.

"She said we're on the front page of the newspaper," Caroline growled, still half asleep. She scooted farther under the covers and tried to go back to sleep.

"Front page of the newspaper!" Chrissy repeated, suddenly awake, throwing off the covers and bounding out of bed. "Come on, Caroline, get up! Our pictures are in the newspaper! Chrissy hurled Caroline's blankets onto the floor and practically yanked her out of bed. "Don't you want to see how you look?" she continued as she pulled on her calico robe. Chrissy pulled Caroline down the hallway and into the Kirby kitchen. "Are we really on the front page?" Chrissy implored as the girls plunked themselves down at the table.

"It's right here," Uncle Richard pointed out, holding up the paper from the kitchen counter where he and Aunt Edith were reading the news item.

"I must admit I didn't recognize you at first," Aunt Edith said. "Then I saw your names printed under the photograph."

"Let me see!" Chrissy cried, grabbing the paper and sticking her nose in the newsprint. "Jumpin' Jiminy!" she exclaimed. "I had no idea we looked so . . ." Chrissy couldn't find the right word.

"Wet." Uncle Richard supplied the correct answer.

"I've never seen either of these outfits," Aunt Edith murmured, pointing at the pictures. "Are they new?"

"Kind of," Chrissy replied in a monotone. "I don't think I'll be wearing mine again. Boy, do we look awful!"

"How awful?" Caroline inquired cautiously.

"Take a look for yourself," Mrs. Kirby told her daughter, motioning her over toward the counter.

"Am I going to be able to live with the experience, or is it going to scar me for life?" Caroline muttered to herself, rubbing her eyes and shuffling toward the group.

"Don't be silly, honey," her mother chuckled.

"It's true you don't look like a debutante, and I can't say much for your escorts, but after all, it is just one picture."

"Think of it as a real-life version of *Swan Lake*," Uncle Richard added, amused by the whole situation.

Caroline's mouth fell open as she gawked at the front page. "I look terrible! Why didn't you tell me how ridiculous I looked?" Caroline nudged Chrissy, who was still checking out her own appearance. "I'll never be able to show my face at school," Caroline said despairingly.

"Are you kidding?" Chrissy interjected. "We may look like drowned rats, but Pete and Nick are also drenched in this picture."

"Supposedly they were saving us, only we didn't need saving," Caroline added. "I look like I have two black eyes," Caroline complained, unable to get over the picture. "Justine will never forgive me for ruining her blouse."

"Look at my hair," said Chrissy. "At least you don't look like a sheepdog."

The foursome laughed and agreed that this would be a story they would all enjoy telling their grandchildren in the years to come.

"Hey, did you read the article itself?" Caroline asked, flipping through the pages of the newspaper.

"I didn't get any further than 'Teen heartthrobs, Pete Becker and Nick Matthews, save fans, Caroline Kirby and Chrissy Madden, from drowning,'" said Uncle Richard.

"You mean there's more," Chrissy said eagerly trying to help Caroline flip the pages.

"Listen to this," Caroline said, sounding bewildered. " 'In order to promote his new film, *Denim Blues*, director Justin Hayes scanned the Bay area for new talent. It was announced that as a publicity stunt, he would "discover" two high school girls to play opposite his stars, Pete Becker and Nick Matthews.' "

"Publicity stunt," Chrissy barked. "What does that mean?"

"It means he never intended to cast any high school girls in his film. It was just a ploy to promote his movie." Caroline slammed down the newspaper and stormed back to the table. "I feel like such a fool."

"They used us to sell tickets." Chrissy's heart sank and she slumped in the chair like a deflated balloon. "They never intended to make us stars, or give us parts in the film?"

"Not for one minute," Caroline snapped.

"But," Chrissy insisted, "everyone was so sincere and helpful."

"Yes, they were, weren't they?" Caroline remarked with a biting edge. "I can't believe we were so stupid."

"You don't think Pete and Nick knew about this, do you?" Chrissy asked.

"Of course they knew, and so did Adam and Josh." Caroline stood up and ran to the bedroom, slamming the door behind her.

"I forgot all about Adam," Chrissy said, looking

to her aunt. "They were really getting close. I can't believe he'd intentionally hurt Caroline."

"Well, she'll never know the truth until she talks to him," Aunt Edith said with a sigh.

"That'll be the day," Chrissy answered with a smirk. "You know how Caroline is when she's angry."

At that moment, the phone rang and Aunt Edith answered it. "Chrissy, it's for Caroline," she said, holding her hand over the receiver. "It's Adam, speaking of the devil."

"I don't think she'll talk to him, but I'll tell her he's on the phone." Chrissy walked slowly to their room, trying to think of something to say that would encourage her cousin to talk to Adam.

"Adam's on the phone and would like to speak with you." Chrissy's voice was quiet and sympathetic as she sat next to a tearful Caroline.

"He had a chance to talk to me before the article came out," Caroline said miserably. "Tell him I'm not home. And don't you talk to him either," she said sternly. Chrissy knew she was serious.

"You'll have to talk to him at some point," Chrissy tried to suggest.

"No, I won't. And I want you to promise me, Christina Madden, that you won't try to intercede or play matchmaker."

"All right—if that's what you really want."

"It is," Caroline said sullenly.

"I'm sorry," Chrissy said, comforting her. "I know how special you thought he was. Let me know if there's anything I can do to help." Chrissy got up and returned quietly to the kitchen, where the phone was still off the hook. Chrissy shook her head no, and indicated to her aunt that she'd also been warned not to talk to him.

"Caroline's not feeling very well right now," Mrs. Kirby said into the phone. "Maybe you can try back later."

For the next few hours, the Kirby household was like Grand Central Station. Justine, Tracy, Maria, and Randy all called, offering their congratulations on the girls' sudden celebrity status. Adam called two more times, but Caroline held her ground and wouldn't leave her room. It wasn't until the doorbell rang in the early afternoon that she finally made an appearance.

"Caroline, come quick," Chrissy called. "Flowers were just delivered for us."

"Who are they from?" Caroline asked.

"Let's read the cards," Chrissy squealed.

Both girls slid the bows off their long white boxes. Chrissy opened hers first and gasped at the sight of twelve long-stemmed yellow roses. "These are the most beautiful flowers I've ever seen," she said, jumping up and down. Quickly she tore open the card, and read it out loud:

Sunshine, please accept these flowers as a token of my appreciation. I'll call later—try to keep tonight free.

Nick

"Can you believe this?" Chrissy said. "Yours must be from Pete."

Caroline slipped off the lid and inhaled the fragrance of a dozen long-stemmed pink roses. "You're right—they're from Pete. I'll bet they're feeling guilty about setting us up."

"Oh, Caroline, don't be such an old shoe. They didn't have to contact us at all. Besides, they were always friendly to us. They didn't encourage us to audition—we did that all on our own."

"I guess you're right," Caroline said, relaxing a little. "They were just doing their jobs."

"And so was Adam."

"I don't want to talk about Adam," she snapped.

"Okay, okay, we won't talk about Adam," Chrissy said. "Why do you think they want us to keep tonight free?"

"Beats me. Maybe they want us to jump off a building so they can take more pictures."

"Quit being so sarcastic. Where would you be if they hadn't come into our lives?"

"Studying, I suppose. I'll try to put my feelings on hold for a while—at least concerning Pete and Nick."

The girls took their flowers and placed them in tall vases. The phone rang for the fiftieth time that day and Chrissy jumped up to answer it.

"If it's Adam . . ." Caroline started.

"I know, I know—you're not available. Kirby residence," Chrissy said. "Hi, Nick," she said, her voice becoming more animated. "The flowers are beautiful. You should smell our living room; it's like a regular garden. . . . Sure, Caroline's here. Get on the phone in the kitchen," she ordered Caroline. "Pete's on the line as well—they want to speak with both of us."

"Okay," Caroline said, perking up and dashing to the kitchen line. "Hello, Pete. The flowers are lovely. Thanks."

The cousins chatted with the guys for a few minutes and then met back in the living room.

"Am I dreaming, or did Nick Matthews just ask me out for dinner at Scoma's?" Chrissy shouted at the top of her lungs. "Wait until the gang hears about this. I'm going to call Maria right now." Chrissy rushed back to the phone and started dialing. Suddenly she slammed down the receiver. "I haven't got a thing to wear!" she cried, looking to Caroline for help.

"Don't look at me. The best outfit I have is still shrinking on the towel rack in the bathroom."

"We've got to look our absolute best tonight," Chrissy said, starting to look desperate.

"Yes, but no more wild, weird clothes," Caroline warned.

"Agreed," Chrissy replied. "We've got to be sophisticated and glamorous."

"Well, that excludes my closet," Caroline remarked, plopping down on the couch.

"Maybe we can get some help from the gang. They might be able to put together something smashing.

"We can try."

"I'll start with Maria," Chrissy said. "She's going to flip."

For the next three hours the Kirby house became a fashion show. Kids Chrissy and Caroline hardly knew from school were coming by to offer everything from prom dresses to bridesmaids' gowns.

Uncle Richard and Aunt Edith had had enough of the pandemonium by two o'clock, and decided to abandon the homefront until seven P.M., when the guys were scheduled to arrive.

"Which one do you like the best, Tracy?" Caroline asked, holding up two very different dresses.

"Definitely the green one," Tracy volunteered.

"No, I think the blue is the best," Maria suggested.

"I never got to see the blue one," Justine said. "Why don't you try it on again?"

"No matter what, I am not trying on another dress," Caroline said, putting her foot down.

"What about this one?" Chrissy asked as she strode into the living room wearing another outfit.

"Chrissy," Maria said, shaking her head and laughing, "you're wearing my red blouse, and Justine's white skirt."

"Oh, for heaven's sake," Chrissy said, sliding to the floor in exhaustion, "I can't try on another dress."

"Do you know what you want to wear?" Justine asked the pair.

"I haven't got the foggiest idea." Chrissy groaned.

"Well, then, I suggest we vote," Maria said excitedly.

"Great idea," Tracy added. "We'll put all the outfits that are wrong or don't fit in the bedroom, and then take the ones we like for Chrissy and put them into the kitchen. Caroline's choices will go here in the living room. Does anyone need to see them modeled before we begin?"

"No," Chrissy and Caroline said in unison.

"Then let's get this place cleaned up, and we can have the judging in half an hour," Maria ordered.

Finally the girls settled on four choices for Caroline and three for Chrissy. The friends walked from room to room, carefully evaluating everything from shoes to accessories. The votes were placed in two separate containers and tabulated by Tracy, who was the scholarship committee's vice-president.

"The vote is unanimous for Chrissy," Tracy proclaimed. She will be wearing the sleeveless black lace prom dress with the white lace tights." The girls cheered their approval and Chrissy was pleased with the committee's selection.

"Can I borrow your pearl earrings, bracelets, and necklace?" Chrissy asked Justine.

"I'd be honored," she replied.

"Now, for Caroline," Tracy said, standing, obviously enjoying her moment in the spotlight. "We have a tie between the green crepe and the royal blue silk with the white tulle wrap. What does everybody think?"

"I have something to say," Caroline interjected.

"You don't get a vote," Tracy teased. "I think the green wins hands down."

"It gets my vote, too," Maria piped up.

"All right, I'll change my vote to the green," Justine grumbled.

"Wait a minute. Who was the fourth vote?" Tracy asked, checking out the papers.

"Me," Chrissy said. "She has to wear the royal blue dress—the green one is too small and she can't zip it up."

"Thank you, Chrissy. I'm glad someone has my best interests in mind. Besides, I like the royal blue one better anyway. It's very chic." Caroline picked up the dress and twirled around the living room. "I think I should wear Justine's black high heels and Tracy's pearls."

"Perfect," Justine said. "Now let's pack up all this other stuff and give these two some time to get ready."

"Holy cow!" Chrissy exclaimed. "It's five o'clock—the guys are picking us up in two hours."

Tracy volunteered to stay and help with hair and makeup. The next hour and a half was serious business. Caroline did her nails, while Chrissy jumped in the shower. Chrissy was relieved when Aunt Edith and Uncle Richard came home, and Aunt Edith chipped in with ironing. Finally, after Tracy tied a pink bow in Chrissy's hair, both girls were ready to step into their gowns.

"I wish I could be Cinderella getting ready for a ball every night." Chrissy sighed.

"Well, those young men are going to be here in fifteen minutes, and I'm not going to let my daughter and my favorite niece go out in their bathrobes," Mr. Kirby announced. The girls laughed and then rushed to their room to finish dressing.

Caroline was ready first and stepped into the living room, where her father stood with his camera, ready to take pictures. Caroline looked elegant in her slim, blue silk dress. The tight-fitting bodice of the dress and the sheer black stockings lent Caroline an elegant look.

"You look beautiful," her mother said, touched.

"They'll be here any minute," Mr. Kirby called. "I want to take some pictures first."

Chrissy made a wobbly entrance, getting used to her heels. Her skin was tanned from all the sun she'd gotten learning how to skateboard, and the full-skirted dress revealed her muscular yet shapely limbs. She modeled her outfit for her applauding aunt and uncle. The large pearl earrings and necklace gave her cast just the right touch.

"You both look lovely," Mrs. Kirby said, giving the girls a hug. Suddenly from down on the street, they heard a loud scream and whistles. They rushed to the window and saw several girls gathered around a stretch limousine that had just pulled up in front of the Kirbys' home.

"I don't believe it!" Chrissy cried, pointing to Justine and Maria, who were waving from the sidewalk.

"It would seem that those fellows are going to have quite a welcoming committee," Mr. Kirby said.

Flashbulbs popped as Pete and Nick stepped out of the car and greeted their fan club.

"This is so exciting," Chrissy said, grabbing Caroline's arm.

"Do you want to answer the door or make an entrance?" Mr. Kirby asked.

"Make an entrance," Chrissy said.

"Open the door!" Caroline cried.

"I'll open the door, and then you can come down the hallway," Mrs. Kirby decided firmly. They all hustled into position just as the buzzer rang.

The introductions went smoothly and Chrissy thought that even Uncle Richard was impressed with the movie idols.

"They'll be home by midnight," Pete stated, shaking Mr. Kirby's hand.

"And I promise that the chauffeur will drive carefully," Nick added. After a few more pictures, the foursome headed downstairs to the hoots and hollers of the scholarship committee.

"This is the most exciting night of my life," Chrissy said to Caroline as they seated themselves in the car. Nick pushed in a cassette and strains of Mozart filled the passengers' compartment.

"What a lovely choice of music," Caroline commented, relaxed in her seat.

"We have some sparkling cider chilling in the bucket. We feel like we owe you an explanation—and a thank you—since you've made our stay in San Francisco so much more exciting," Pete said.

"We just wished that your director would have been honest about his intentions," Caroline stated.

"Unfortunately, that's show biz," Nick added. "We didn't even know it was a hoax until after we made the announcement about the upcoming auditions at your school."

"What about the rest of your staff?" Chrissy questioned, knowing that Caroline was dying to ask.

"Justin's so unpredictable that most of them had no idea he wasn't on the level, until the morning of the audition when he told us our shooting schedule," Pete said apologetically.

"That could explain why someone would be helpful and supportive up to the very last minute," Chrissy said softly.

Caroline was quiet during the ride over the Golden Gate Bridge. Chrissy knew that she was thinking about Adam, and wanted to talk to him.

"You can call him later," Chrissy whispered to her cousin. "I'm sure he'll understand."

"Thanks for asking," Caroline said.

"Hey, how about a movie? This car has a VCR," Josh said, opening the window of the cab.

"What are you doing here?" Chrissy said, giggling.

"Sometimes I double as chauffeur," Josh answered. "Hey, I heard about your skateboarding at the restaurant. I understand it was quite a show."

Chrissy tried to cover her embarrassment, but just then the guys poured the cider. As the limo whisked across the Golden Gate Bridge to Sausalito, Nick and Pete made several toasts in Chrissy's and Caroline's honor.

Chapter 15

The sun dangled over the bridge like a bright red Christmas ornament hung from a tree. Chrissy pinched her arm, just to remind herself that the date was really happening. She felt like Cinderella going to the ball, and just like in the fairy tale, it was going to be over at midnight. *It doesn't matter anymore that we're not going to be in the movie*, Chrissy thought. She guessed that the real reason she had wanted to do the film was to meet Pete and Nick. They weren't like movie stars at all, Chrissy decided. They were people, like everyone else. Nick looked uncomfortable in his coat and tie, Chrissy thought, smiling, and Pete was out of place without a book and some glasses.

"Here we are," Josh called through the open

window. "And it looks like we've got another welcoming committee. Do you want me to dodge them and drop you off at the side entrance?"

Pete groaned and slid down into his seat, while Nick covered his face with his left hand. "Nope," Nick said, "I think our dates should see what it's like to live in the limelight."

"You're right," Pete said, sitting up straight. "Besides, these are the most attractive dates we've ever had."

"Why, thank you, Pete," Caroline said, smiling widely.

"You won't hear any complaints from me," Chrissy cheered, primping herself for the arrival. "How do you think they knew we were coming?"

"Knowing Justin, or rather one of Justin's spies, the information was leaked and our secret plans foiled," Pete surmised.

"Or it could be that Chrissy and I blabbed it to everyone we know."

"We didn't know whether or not we should keep it a secret," Chrissy admitted.

"Don't worry about it," Nick reassured her. "We'll give them the full treatment, right, girls?"

"Sure," Chrissy said. "This is the most exciting thing that's ever happened to me."

"All right, then," Josh said, pulling into the restaurant parking lot, "hold on to your hats." Chrissy and Caroline squealed with excitement.

Josh knew what to do. He slowly circled the lot so the fans had enough time to get into position. Then he jumped out of the car and opened the door for the girls to make their entrance. Unfortunately, it didn't go quite as either girl had imagined it. Mobs of screaming girls pressed against them like a tight-fitting glove. Before they knew it, they had been shuffled to one side, away from Nick, Pete, and the limo. After what seemed like an eternity, the guys finished signing autographs and made their way to the entrance, where Chrissy and Caroline stood waiting.

"Sorry to keep you waiting so long," Nick apologized.

"I hate those mobs," Pete said, wiping his forehead with a handkerchief. "Sometimes it takes us over an hour to get into the grocery store."

"That's awful!" Caroline exclaimed. "Why don't they leave you alone?"

"That's show biz," Nick said.

"Well, I feel like yesterday's garbage," Chrissy whispered to Caroline as they finally moved into the reception area.

"Good evening," the maître d' said, recognizing the pair. "your table is ready."

"Thanks a lot," Pete said, slipping him a bill. "Do you think you could arrange for some privacy?"

"I will be most happy to," he replied.

Chrissy stood over by one side to soak in the ambience of the elegant restaurant. Along the far wall were long, glass windows facing the bridge and San Francisco Bay. The atmosphere was dark, yet cozy, with a nautical flair of ropes and lanterns. The foursome was escorted to a table overlooking the water.

"What a beautiful view," Caroline said as she sat down in a chair.

"I like my view better," Pete complimented her. Chrissy smiled as she watched Caroline evaluate her date. She could read her cousin like a book. Chrissy knew that Caroline was flattered by Pete, but the glow that Caroline got in the presence of Adam just wasn't here.

"Well, sunshine," Nick said, grinning, "what would you like to have for dinner?"

Chrissy opened the large menu and scanned all the delicacies. "I've gotten better at dining out since I arrived in San Francisco," Chrissy confessed, "but I'm still not sure what half the things are—or if I really want to know."

"I'll tell you what, then. Why don't you let me order for you? Then after the meal I'll tell you what you had."

"As long as it isn't octopus eyes, or something like that."

"It's a deal," Nick said. "We'll let Pete order the appetizers and I'll order the entrées."

"May I take your order?" the waitress asked, blushing as she recognized her patrons. "I'd love an autograph, too," she whispered. "I know you don't want to be bothered, but if you could just sign here."

"No problem," said Nick as he scribbled on the paper napkin.

The dinner was the most elegant that Chrissy

had ever eaten. For appetizers Pete had ordered escargots and fresh smelts. Chrissy loved the snails, but she thought the smelts were slimy. The main course consisted of lobster tails. Chrissy savored each buttery bite of the seafood, the twice-baked potatoes, and the Caesar salad. Chrissy wasn't sure she'd saved enough room for dessert, but when the tiny *pots de crèmes* arrived at the table, she knew they were too good to pass up.

"These are absolutely incredible," she declared as the last chocolate mouthful melted down her throat. "I think I'll burst if I try to eat anything for the rest of the week."

"Before we have coffee," Pete started to explain, "I just want to say on behalf of Nick and myself that we really appreciate all that you've put up with during these past few weeks. I know Justin shouldn't have gotten your hopes up about the movie, and I just want to say I'm sorry. You were great sports."

"We've had a great time," Chrissy said. "I wouldn't have changed a thing . . . well, maybe a few things."

"Like the two of us not talking to each other," said Caroline.

"And aching from all those skateboard spills," Chrissy added.

"Not to mention—" Nick started to say.

"I know you're out on a date," a young girl said, "but do you think I could have your autograph?" Nick and Pete smiled politely and started to

reach for the girl's book. "Not *your* autographs,"
the girl added, "the *girls'*."

"Mine?" Chrissy asked. "What do you want my
autograph for?"

"Because I saw your picture in the newspaper.
That means you must be famous."

"I'd be happy to sign your book," Chrissy
announced, beaming.

"Me, too," Caroline stated, signing with a flair.

Chrissy hated to see her glorious evening coming to a close, but she knew the witching hour
was close at hand. Before they left, Nick pointed
out his favorite fishing spot in the cove and
promised he'd take her along if they ever came
back to San Francisco. Chrissy noticed that Pete
and Caroline had taken up right where they had
left off at the end of their last conversation.
Caroline was explaining a passage in a poem
she'd read last week, and Pete gave Caroline the
name of an amazing book he'd just finished
reading. They paid the bill and thanked the
proprietor for his help. A few more waitresses
asked for autographs, so Chrissy and Caroline
excused themselves and went to the ladies'
lounge.

"Any word from Adam?" Chrissy asked cautiously.

"How did you know I was thinking about him?"
Caroline asked, surprised.

"I know you pretty well, Cara, and besides, you
excused yourself twice during dinner to use the
phone."

"How do you know I left the table to use the phone?"

"Because you looked disappointed each time you came back."

"Oh, dear," Caroline said. "Do you think Pete noticed?"

"Nah, I think I could tell, but no one else could. You must really like him."

"I do," Caroline admitted. "I didn't realize how much until tonight. Pete's a great guy, but he's just not Adam. Everything I look at reminds me of Adam." Her eyes became misty, and Chrissy was sure her cousin was going to cry.

"Why don't you try him once more before we leave?" Chrissy suggested. She combed her hair and touched up her lipstick, while she waited for Caroline to complete her call. "Any luck this time?" Chrissy asked when they met outside the ladies' room.

"No, and Mom said he hasn't tried all evening." Her eyes filled with tears and she looked worried, and about to cry.

"I'm sure he's just out for the evening or something. We'll sit on his doorstep tomorrow if that's what it takes."

"I'm really having a good time with Pete and Nick, but I think I want to go home."

"Me, too." Chrissy sighed. "I'm not sure I'm ready to be a movie star yet. My face hurts from smiling all the time."

The girls met the boys outside the restaurant, where they were again mobbed by fans and autograph seekers. Finally, they were able to squeeze into the car.

"Sometimes they even try to tear our clothes off," Nick said. Chrissy blushed, and Nick reassured her that he was joking by taking her hand.

Josh opened the sun roof, and Chrissy caught a glimpse of the stars. Quickly she made a wish. *Star light, star bright, first star I see tonight.* She closed her eyes and made a wish, praying that it would come true.

Before she knew it, the limo was traveling down Lombard Street, and then pulling up in front of the Kirbys' apartment house near Nob Hill. Chrissy felt nervous as Nick got out and opened the door. It felt like a real date—not so much like a date with a movie star, she thought, but a date with a boy she liked because he was a nice, fun person. Gently, Nick put his arm around Chrissy's shoulder and started to lead her to the doorstep. Chrissy felt her heartbeat quicken, as she tenderly rested her head on his shoulder and Nick smiled back, giving Chrissy a hug. It was the first time that they'd been alone all evening and Nick seemed to be enjoying it as much as she was. The air was warm and the sky was a dark midnight blue.

"I had a really good time tonight," Nick whispered as he turned Chrissy to face him.

"So did I," Chrissy replied.

"Thanks for showing me what it's like to go on a date with a genuinely nice girl." With that Nick bent down toward Chrissy. Their lips met and

Chrissy was sure that she heard fireworks. He kissed her again—the kiss was warm and lingering this time—and then he slowly descended the steps and disappeared into the car.

Though she was in a dreamlike state, Chrissy noticed Caroline walking with a boy on the hill in front of the house. At first she thought it was Pete, but when she saw the glow on Caroline's face, she could see that it was Adam. He must have been waiting outside for them to get back. Chrissy smiled and wrapped her arms around herself.

"My wishes do come true," she whispered to herself, walking in the front door.

Here's a sneak preview of *Big Sister*, book number eleven in the continuing SUGAR & SPICE series from Ivy Books.

"He's staying *here*?" Chrissy shrieked. She wasn't sure whether her Aunt Edith's news filled her with a sudden surge of horror or joy. Her younger brother Will would be living with her and the Kirbys and attending Maxwell High— how would she survive?

"But mother," Caroline said, "we don't have room for a teenage boy. You can't put anyone else in my room," she said firmly before anyone even suggested it.

"Of course not, dear," her mother said calmly. "I wouldn't room a fifteen-year-old boy with two seventeen-year-old girls. We'll simply block off a portion of the dining room into a makeshift bedroom for Will."

"Does Will want to live here?" Chrissy asked her parents.

"We don't know yet, honeybun," her mother said. "It was your Aunt Edith's idea. . ."

Caroline shot an indignant look at her mother, and Chrissy could sympathize. Just a few minutes ago, Chrissy had felt bad that Will was returning to Iowa with her parents after such a short Christmas visit. But having her little brother at Maxwell High was another story altogether!

ABOUT THE AUTHOR

Janet Quin-Harkin is the author of more than thirty books for young adults, including the best-selling *Ten-Boy Summer* and *On Our Own*, its sequel series. Ms. Quin-Harkin lives just outside of San Francisco with her husband, three teenage daughters, and one son.